THE GREY HORDE CREEPS

CREEPS

By Grant Stockbridge

I0617771

STEEGER BOOKS • 2021

© 1938, 2021 Argosy Communications, Inc. All rights reserved.

THE SPIDER® is a trademark of Argosy Communications, Inc.
Authorized and produced under license.

PUBLISHING HISTORY

"The Grey Horde Creeps" originally appeared in the March 1938 (Vol. 14, No. 2)
issue of *The Spider* magazine. Copyright 2021 by Argosy Communications, Inc.
All rights reserved.

ALL RIGHTS RESERVED

No part of this book may be reproduced or utilized in any form or by any means, electronic or mechanical, without permission in writing from the publisher.

This edition has been marked via subtle changes, so anyone who reprints from this collection is committing a violation of copyright.

Visit STEEGERBOOKS FOR more books like this.

THE SPIDER:
THE GREY HORDE CREEPS

CHAPTER 1
DEATH COMES AT NIGHT

JUMBLED HILLS showed black against a starless sky. On the road that angled, ghostly grey, across the valley, a spot of red light gleamed an instant, winked out, shone again. The drone of an airplane engine, muttering overhead, sharpened, then faded. Abruptly, blue-white glare broke out from a landing flare, swinging high up on its miniature parachute.

Where the red light had shone a figure stood, arms folded, impassive—a man with his head bound in a white Eastern turban. About him, inky-black shadows swung and danced as the flare drifted lower. Then into its glare, an autogiro plane dropped swiftly, its rotors fantastic as some antediluvian beast's wings. Its shadow skimmed the ground beneath, then shadow and plane merged, the flare's light pinched out—and the autogiro was motionless on the earth. Its motor whispered, idling. Instantly, a man sprang from the cabin cockpit, set to work to fold back the rotors parallel above the plane's body. His body was lithe; his movements had a studied, swift efficiency.

"Quickly, Ram Singh!" he called softly into the shadows, the timber of his voice vibrant with command. "I was followed by another plane. I'm sure of it!"

From the darkness, the turbaned man stepped into the faint light glow from the 'giro's instrument panel. "There is need to hurry, *sahib!*" his harsh, strong voice answered. "There are

1

No mortal beings could survive
such slashing butchery!

strange things in that town—things more of the demon land than human!"

For an instant, the other man paused. His face thrust forward

into the minute glow, hawk-like, with its thin-bridged, strong nose, the flat-planed angular cheeks.

"You afraid, Ram Singh!" he said, mockery in his voice. "Thou, my brave warrior!"

Ram Singh stiffened. "Has thy servant ever failed Wentworth

sahib?" he demanded. "I am thy servant through hell itself… I follow where my lord leads."

Wentworth remained in that glow of light an instant longer, his eyes searching the Sikh's bearded face. It was strange—the thing which he had caught in the fearless Hindu's voice. It was still there—he had not been mistaken. The thing was fear. "Make haste," he ordered curtly.

THERE WAS a vertical crease between Richard Wentworth's keen grey eyes as he finished the swift conversion of the plane into a road-running vehicle. Such jobs were sold commercially, but his was especially constructed and capable of seventy miles an hour on the road. As Ram Singh ducked into the cabin, Wentworth engaged the engine to the wheels, and the curious ship lurched forward.

"Report," he ordered.

Ram Singh's voice was formal, offended. "Following the *sahib's* orders, his servant came to Hillville to investigate the case of the vanished *hakim*. I assumed the role of a gypsy fortune-teller and learned more than I told."

Wentworth's mind, leaping ahead, pieced in the story. More than five hundred men had disappeared in the Kentucky hill towns. Most of them had gone off alone and never reappeared; sometimes two, together, would drop out of sight. Individually, these cases seemed unimportant, and local police gave them only desultory attention. But to Wentworth, perpetually alert for any fresh outbreak of criminal conspiracy, the collective picture was alarming. He suspected that a sinister intelligence was responsible. Three nights ago, his suspicions had been confirmed—to his entire satisfaction.

A group of ten men, working in a logging camp, had vanished in a single night without leaving a trace! Hard on the heels of this report had come the news of a Dr. Conoly Rand, who had departed upon a night call and never returned. Police had arrested a garage worker—suitor for Rand's daughter—and Wentworth had sent Ram Singh to investigate. But now the Sikh's reference to "demons" puzzled Wentworth.

"You mentioned demons," Wentworth cut in.

"Han, sahib!" Ram Singh muttered and fell silent.

Wentworth threw a sharp glance at him, peered upward through the glass roof of the ship—and swore softly under his breath. Too often had he seen the exhaust flow of a plane against the night sky not to recognize the roseate glow he detected now. He was still being followed! If he had needed any further confirmation of his fears, here it was!

"Thy servant could take the ship to the hideaway in darkness," Ram Singh volunteered.

Without a word, Wentworth cut off the lights, stopped and slid over as Ram Singh swiftly circled to the driver's seat. Why was Ram Singh so curiously reluctant to talk of the demons—or whatever it was he had seen that had aroused his Eastern superstitions? The Sikh's reluctance was more ominous to Wentworth than any babbling fear might have been.

Under Ram Singh's guidance, the ship sprang ahead, jerking and jarring along a roughening road. The night was utterly black but the trees, growing ever closer along the sides of the road, showed a pale gap of sky overhead. It was by this Ram Singh steered. Presently, the Sikh began to talk in his native Punjabi—as always when under the hard stress of emotion. Wentworth's chiseled face drew into longer lines as he listened.

"One woman," Ram Singh said, "the daughter of Rand *hakim*, has seen the demons—and she only. On the night her father disappeared, she and her lover—"

"His name?" Wentworth cut in.

"John Dawson *sahib*," Ram Singh said. "These two were worried when Rand *hakim* did not return, and went seeking him. The man walked up a foot-trail to a cabin, and the woman drove on to a place where she could turn the car. On that trail, she saw… two of the demons."

Ram Singh's voice died, and Wentworth glanced at him sharply. The jut of the Sikh's beard showed the hard compression of his lips. Wentworth held his peace, peered upward at the skies. The plane was questing back toward his landing place now. **ABRUPTLY, A** blue-white illumination spilled down over the jumbled landscape—the ship had released a landing flare! Without orders, Ram Singh jammed the 'giro to the side of the road beneath the black shadow of a tree. They sat, peering upward with bitterly watchful eyes.

Danger was no new thing to these two. Death was a familiar foeman upon whom they could look fearlessly, though with respect. In such a life as Wentworth lived, this attitude was inevitable, for long ago he had pledged his life to ceaseless warfare against crime—a warfare, in itself, outside the law. Wentworth had seen too many insolently guilty criminals escape the courts through the safeguards set up to protect the innocent from persecution. And those criminals had learned to dread the swift justice meted out in his secret identity of the Spider!

The drone of the pursuing plane was plainly audible now as it swung lower, but Wentworth judged that no landing was planned. They were seeking him! He frowned. How in heaven's name could criminals have spotted his purpose so soon? Or was it merely that this entire area was patrolled from the skies! The ship roared overhead at a few hundred feet, banked sharply.

"Fast!" Wentworth ordered. "They've spotted us!"

The 'giro leaped forward, bouncing wildly. The flare sank lower, behind the trees, throwing bands of blue-white brilliance and inky shadow across the road... then blotted out. Overhead, the plane had banked again and was skimming back over the road.

"They'll attack," Wentworth said abruptly. "Is there a side-road—or even a lane into the woods?"

Ram Singh grunted, braked and spun into a rough woods track that was half overgrown with shrubbery. An instant later, he slammed on brakes and frantically fought the wheel—in vain. The 'giro lifted on the breath of a crashing explosion, slammed its nose against a tree-trunk. For an instant, the entire scene stood out vividly around them. Jagged spears of crimson and yellow flame stabbed upward at the heavens, and Wentworth felt his ears go dead with concussion! Momentum hurled him violently forward against the instrument panel. He barely managed to cushion his forehead with his hands.

Even so, he was partly stunned and huddled limply on the floor of the cockpit while he fought to collect his numbed senses. He was aware of fierce hands seizing him, then being carried on a wild, reeling course through the underbrush. Presently, the crashing of it penetrated his deafened ear-drums. With it came Ram Singh's voice, pleading.

"Master! Master!" he sobbed. "They will overtake us, unless...."

So it was Ram Singh who carried him—but in Heaven's name, why?

"I can walk," Wentworth said thickly.

Instantly, he was on his feet, and Ram Singh's powerful hand closed on his biceps, dragging him forward at a furious pace.

"Quickly, master!" the Sikh pleaded. "Quickly, the demons are all about us!"

In spite of his impatience with Eastern superstition, Wentworth felt coldness touch his scalp.

"Nonsense!" he muttered, but he ran stumblingly at Ram Singh's direction.

In the darkness, they blundered over the bank of a low ravine and, in its bottom, plunged into icy water above their knees.

"Turn up the creek," Wentworth ordered. He fished out a flashlight and, hooding it with his hands, threw a faint glow upon the creek-bed. For a hundred yards, they fled up its course, then crouched under an overhanging bank. The water was almost waist-deep here and plucked and tugged at their legs.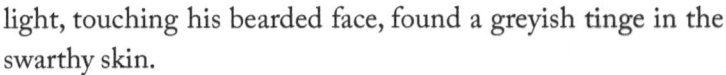

"Now," Wentworth said shortly, "what is this nonsense about demons? Speak up!"

Ram Singh folded his arms across his chest, and Wentworth's shielded light, touching his bearded face, found a greyish tinge in the swarthy skin.

"Now by the One True God!" Ram Singh muttered hoarsely.

"All right," Wentworth said quietly, "My apologies, Ram Singh. Thou hast never evaded truth nor hast thou faltered in battle. Thou are a Singh—a lion. Whatever thou sayeth I believe."

Ram Singh touched hand to heart and forehead, humbly. "What thy servant sayeth is truth…" He hesitated. "This woman, the daughter of Rand *hakim*, on the country road, saw two… creatures who were huge and white and naked. When her head-lights struck them, she stopped, but they screamed and rushed toward her. She ran into them. She knocked them both to the ground and her car ran over one. When she drove on, as rapidly as possible over the rough road, those two still pursued her. Neither had been harmed by her car, although it was large and heavy." He took a breath.

"As she drove, she heard another scream behind her, and afterward she saw them no more. It was as if they had vanished with that scream. This was her story, *sahib.*"

WENTWORTH FROWNED, staring into the dark-

9

ness that pressed close about them—a darkness that gave forth no sound save the gurgle of the water about their hips and the overhead drone of that questing, deadly plane.

"You believed that story?" he said quietly. After all, there was small reason in this for the Sikh's terror.

"No, *sahib*," said Ram Singh, "nor did anyone else. But I examined the woman's car, and she had struck something that was… I found fragments of white skin on her fenders and hairs that were white—coarse and white as is the hair of beasts!"

Wentworth swore softly, fighting once more against that tingle of cold across his scalp.

"And, master," Ram Singh went on hoarsely, "tonight when I came to meet you, I saw such creatures in the woods. In the light of the bomb they stood in the road before us—four… creatures, huge and white and naked! Even now, they must be questing the woods for us, smelling out our spoor!"

Quiet confidence was in Wentworth's voice as he answered— the voice of a man accustomed to act coolly. "We have our guns, and your long, sharp knives, Ram Singh!"

Ram Singh's answer was steady. "Master, on that skin that I found, there was no blood."

Relief flooded into Wentworth's soul even while that reply puzzled him. Bloodless demons were supposed, in the Punjabi superstition, to haunt the mountain fastnesses. Now, at last, he had his answer—but it was an answer that settled only the basic reason of Ram Singh's undoubted fear. His own mind gave him no explanation of how such things, as Ram Singh described, could be. His ears took up the strain of the watch in which his eyes could not help. Here in the Kentucky hills, many things were dark and hidden. There were vast areas a man might traverse only on horseback and afoot; there were people who, for generations had been cut off from the world....

Wentworth's keen mind told him that somewhere in the disappearance of Dr. Conoly Rand he might find a clue. The man was well known in the world of science for his ethnological papers. No one knew why he had buried himself in these hills from which he had sprung. What made his disappearance significant was that, of all the five hundred cases of which Wentworth had taken notice, Dr. Rand was the only man of educated background.

"We must reach Hillville," Wentworth said shortly, his voice a bare whisper.

Ram Singh answered in the same way. "Two miles from here on a side road, I hid a car. It may be that it is still there."

Wentworth glanced toward the Sikh sharply, but Ram Singh was not thinking now of demon things. It was a fact that a trap had been set for them—and that might have well caused the discovery of the car.

"We will go to it," Wentworth directed quietly. Ram Singh's *salaam* of assent was immediate, and he surged through the clutching waters of the creek toward the opposite bank. Wentworth followed, his ears alert for any sound behind them, while his mind quested.

"There is a farmhouse near here," he said abruptly. "I saw it from the air. There is no time now to hunt for the car and fight our way clear, if there is a trap there. Dr. Rand's daughter—we must reach her at once!"

Ram Singh halted, and the black loom of his body beside Wentworth was a silent resignation of leadership.

"Cross the main road," Wentworth said curtly, "then back about a half a mile—and hurry!"

Ram Singh lunged out in a tireless lope that he could continue for half a day without rest. As he ran, he dropped back whispered words. "Thy servant has been careless!"

"No," Wentworth replied. "It was your entrance into this territory that betrayed us. But now they have connected you with the fortune-teller of Hillville! And they will... remove the girl!"

Ram Singh's stride lengthened. Wentworth's lips set in grim resolve. Damn it, why had he waited so long to join the battle! He needed no more than this night's encounter to convince him that he was opposed by a closely organized criminal force. And these demons-

Ram Singh's voice floated back to him in a hoarse croak. "Run, master! Run for your life! The demons are... behind us!"

Even as the Sikh gasped the warning, Wentworth heard the cry—a rising, harsh scream, like the hunting cry of some fierce predatory beast!

CHAPTER 2
THROUGH THE DARKNESS

IT WAS a curious thing to Wentworth that, though his mind was unafraid, coldness should course over his body at the mere sound of that awful cry. Ram Singh's stride had stretched out until he fairly flew over the ground. An instant later, they burst out into the road and whipped back the way they had come. They ran softly in the dry dust that edged the highway.

Something primitive in Wentworth urged him to turn back and fight, but, as always, the cold precision of his mind dominated. They might win in a battle with these demons of Ram Singh's—it would be extraordinary if such trained fighters as himself and the Sikh should not—but they would lose precious time. At that farmhouse there must be some means of travel—horses if not an automobile. They *must* reach Hillville!

Once more, the hunting scream rang out behind them, but Wentworth, hopefully, thought that it was farther away.

"Into the woods now," he panted.

Ram Singh swerved and, an instant later, they were in the black shadows. The woods were more open here, pine trees whose thick-needled tops soughed mournfully in the faint night wind. Underfoot was soft with dead needles, slippery beneath hard leather soles. They sped on—debouched suddenly into a plowed field where young corn just thrust its spears above the earth. A quarter mile away, the black bulk of the farmhouse showed. They lunged toward it. The thick, plowed earth of the fields clung to their feet like gripping hands. Wentworth's lungs labored. Even the stalwart Ram Singh's breath sounded hoarsely, whistling through distended nostrils.

The drone of the murderous plane overhead became louder, but Wentworth dared not take time to search for the faint trace of its exhaust glow. If a landing flare were dropped now, it would doom them.

"Straight into the house!" he ordered.

They fought clear of the plowed ground, struck easier going on turf, slanted past a single, twisted elm and hammered for the porchless door. Abruptly, Ram Singh threw up an arm and skidded to a halt. The door gaped open, battered from its hinges. Across the sill lay the body of what had been a woman....

Wentworth stared and felt rage strike red-hot through his veins.

"Do you believe now, master," gasped Ram Singh, "in demons?"

"To the barn," Wentworth snapped, but Ram Singh's words rang in his brain as he sprinted on. Demons! Surely, no human being could do to that woman... what had been done to her. As they circled the house, light sprang once more from the heavens—as menacing to them as machine-gun bullets. Wentworth seized Ram Singh's arm, and they crouched close against the wall of the house while the glare of another landing flare struck brutally at the earth.

Wentworth's mind was in turmoil. The things he had experienced tonight fitted into no orderly pattern. Men had disappeared, a woman had been mauled to death. Demons hunted the woods with the screams of hunting beasts—and overhead a modern airplane attacked another ship with bombs for no more reason than an admittedly mysterious landing in the hills! It could be no more than that. They could not know that he was—the Spider! Wentworth was crouched like a sprinter at the mark,

as the flare glided toward earth. The
instant darkness fell again, he hurled
himself toward the barn.

A cry of relief welled from his lips,
as he burst into the darkness. That
black hulk was an automobile of
some sort. Whether or not there was
a key, he could have it started within
minutes. He lunged for the driver's
seat, climbed behind the wheel of an
antiquated Dodge, fumbled at the
dashboard. No key. With an oath, he
switched on the flashlight and fumbled for tools beneath the
seat; attacked the wiring.

"Watch at the door, Ram Singh!" he ordered.

Minutes dragged past while he hacked at steel sheathed ignition wires. The heavy beating of his heart marked off the seconds,
and they seemed endless. Perspiration slid down into his eyes,
but at last he had completed the link. He kicked the starter, and
the motor bellowed noisily into life. Instantly, Ram Singh was
beside him, taking over the wheel.

"Make it the straight road to Hillville," Wentworth snapped.
"Our only safety lies in speed. No lights."

THE CAR lurched backward, was wrenched in a curve and
straightened out for the road. The hunch of the Sikh's shoulders
was belligerent. The road ahead, both knew, would be blocked
by... by what? Wentworth shook his head. This talk of bloodless
demons was ridiculous. But he, himself, had heard the scream,

and could believe literally in Ram Singh's description of what he had seen and heard.

Wentworth cursed softly at the car's lumbering progress. At top speed, on a good road, it might reach fifty miles an hour. Its best now was somewhere near thirty-five. Ahead, now, was the black pit of the bomb crater. Wentworth estimated swiftly that there would be just room to skirt its edge to the right. They were within a hundred feet of it when figures burst from the woods—white, amorphous figures that at first seemed human. There was a bestial slope to the shoulders, a crouching posture in the walk, but the human shape was there—and they walked on two legs. There were four, five… a dozen of them, bursting, one after another, from the woods and crowding into that narrow isthmus which the car must travel.

"Lights!" Wentworth snapped.

The headlights reached out feebly, yellow and dim. Wentworth's automatic thudded into his palm. He weighed it, and waited. Ram Singh was jockeying the last notch of speed from the wreck of a car. In their path, the pack gibbered and danced. They tossed threatening hands into the air and their screams were the screams of beasts! Wentworth had only a brief glance of their queer, white, twisted shapes, then he was shooting.

His aim was a deadly thing, and even the jouncing of the car could not spoil it. He threw lead at the nearest of the creatures and knew his bullet went home, for the thing reeled backward a step. Then, with a scream that ached in Wentworth's ears, the beast-man charged the car! In his hand now glittered a long, heavy machete-like blade!

16

Deliberately, Wentworth squeezed out another bullet—and still the creature charged on! Nor could Wentworth detect any trace of blood upon its chest!

Ram Singh's bearded lips were writhing with strange Punjabi curses, harsh as his native hills. His hands on the wheel showed knuckles white from strain. But he held the car firmly in line. There was a jarring crash as the radiator of the machine slammed against the charging demon. The gleaming knife flew straight forward from his hand, glanced off the metal frame of the top and slit the canvas within inches of Wentworth's head. For a fraction of a second, the out-reaching, brutal fingers clawed at the radiator cap, then he was tossed aside.

Wentworth wrenched his head about, saw the thing scramble to its feet again—and come after them, screaming! *It came after them with two bullets in its vitals, after a blow that must have smashed the life instantly from a man!*

Wentworth realized that curses were pouring from his own lips, his hand white where he gripped the dashboard as a brace— and coldness raced over his limbs. It was ridiculous, unbelievable. And yet this incredible nightmare had occurred before his own eyes!

THE CAR was shuddering onward, charging toward the other creatures who still thronged that narrow pass. Wentworth lifted his automatic, hesitated, then deliberately opened fire again. This time he did not shoot at their bodies, but at their legs. Bullets might not stop them, but he had never yet seen any two-legged creature that could run on a broken leg! His first shot punched the leg out from under one of the beasts! It went

RICHARD WENTWORTH .

down, surged up again on that one good leg and began to hop forward, swinging its murderous blade, screaming—while that bullet-broken leg flapped grotesquely, horribly.

Into the midst of that tangle of living creatures, the car

charged. Several were tossed aside. The car lurched, slipped sideways toward the bomb crater. The bodies under the wheels seemed to be clinging with living hands to slow it down, to overthrow it into that hole. Grimly, Ram Singh fought the wheel, pumped gas to the cylinders. The motor roared in second gear. A knife struck the glass, and glittering shards slashed like shrapnel against Wentworth's chest and hurriedly up-thrown arm.

His automatic was empty. He lunged into the tonneau of the car, caught up the knife that had been hurled there and wielded it like a saber. It sliced through the arm of one of the creatures—and no gush of blood answered it.

The car shuddered, almost stationary, and the creatures flung themselves on the running-board, hacking with their knives. Only the steel frame of the top—the fact that they apparently did not know enough to thrust with the blades—saved Wentworth and Ram Singh from instant death. Wentworth was slashing wildly, hacking at arms, at chests and heads. Ram Singh was protected because the crater gaped at his very elbow. The

car lurched as a wheel slipped to the edge. The tires whined and smoked, gripped—lost hold, gripped again.

Wentworth could not have told at what moment the car began to lurch forward again. It was a welter of slashing, fearful butchery. Killing, he could not call it, for even those whose limbs he severed, clawed at the car with bloodless stumps. It must have been the added weight of those bodies which enabled the tires finally to grip and ease them past the crater.

God, they *were* demons! No mortal beings could survive such slashing butchery as that which greeted those who came at Ram Singh's unprotected left. Frantically, he fought for speed from the engine and the car slowly picked up headway. One of the white beasts flung itself on the left running-board, reached beneath the top and started a slashing blow at Ram Singh's back. Wentworth whipped his own blade in a curtailed arc, a chopping saber slash. The hand and knife dropped to the floor inside the car, but the stump of the arm continued its blow, prodded Ram Singh violently in the back of the neck... until the body fell off.

Ram Singh slumped forward over the wheel. Instantly, Wentworth yanked the Sikh from behind the wheel, vaulted into the seat and slammed the accelerator to the floor.

The car groaned and hammered, as he forced the last notch of speed from the engine. He knew the general direction of Hillville, but the road, itself, was strange to him. Ram Singh slouched like a dead man on the seat. Now, once more, even through the racket of the engine, Wentworth heard the whining roar of a diving plane! He clicked off the lights. They were too dim to be of much value, anyhow, and at least he would not provide the plane with an accurate target. His shoulders were hunched, waiting for the expected bomb-blast... but none came. THE PLANE zipped overhead, darted a mile or more ahead and dropped a landing flare, then whirled back. Wentworth's lips twisted in a harsh smile. He had no weapons save his wits with which to oppose the devastating force of those bombs. The darkness of the night was of small value when the road could be lighted so vividly by those flares. But there must be an end of them sometime, as there must be an end of the bombs. If he could stall....

But there could be no delay. Behind him, the white demons still pressed on in pursuit and ahead... He must find the doctor's daughter first! If the criminals, who were masters of the beast-men, would strike so terribly on mere suspicion, they would not hesitate to follow Ram Singh's backtrail—and wipe out any contact there which might betray them. Wentworth frowned as he sped on. Could he be sure that there was criminal dominance here? He shook the question from his mind. The plane was behind him, swooping down. Wentworth stood on the brake and the ancient car slued wildly sideways, tried to climb the ditch.

Against the white glare of the flare, Wentworth spotted the flickering dark shadow of the falling bomb, not a hundred feet ahead. He covered his ears, bowed forward over the wheel. The hurricane of the blast swept over him, left him reeling, half-senseless, yet one roweling thought was in his mind. He must get under way instantly or the next bomb would catch him stationary. He ground the car out of the ditch, went reeling down the road. His senses were still numbed, but he concentrated on finding the bomb crater; managed to skirt it and pushed on.

He twisted his dizzy head back to peer up toward the sky and discovered that the blast had swept the top completely off the car. Beside him, Ram Singh stirred weakly, pushed himself erect. Another bomb, striking behind the car, sent it staggering. Ram Singh stared about with a stiffly turning head. His voice came out thickly.

"One quarter mile ahead, *sahib*. Narrow road to the right." He slumped down, gripping his head.

Wentworth concentrated all his strength on reaching that road. It was a narrow road… and—staring ahead—he could see that it would lead through woods. On such a lane as that, they would be invisible to the swooping death from the skies. Once more before he reached the turnoff, a bomb shattered the night and half-stunned Wentworth. But he made the turnoff, and soon the car was leaping and bounding down a steep grade between in-pressing embankments. After a mile of that, the car lunged out onto a wider road and Wentworth glimpsed a sign—

HILLVILLE—5 M.

From his swift questions, hurled at Ram Singh, he learned that Dr. Rand's home was on the near side of the town. The daughter, named Janet, would be at the house, Ram Singh thought. John Dawson had that day been released, for lack of evidence, and had announced his intention of standing guard over Janet Rand, though everyone else had laughed at her story of the white demons.

"You'll tell me the turns to take," Wentworth said finally. "Reload the guns. Ammunition in my right-hand pocket."

Ram Singh sat very stiffly while his hands moved mechanically about their task.

"Master," he said hesitantly "will you swear to me those… those creatures were not demons?"

Wentworth opened his lips, hesitated, then swore angrily. "I swear to you, they are not, Ram Singh," he said, "but it is a thing I could not prove. I *know* there are no such things as demons. But those white beasts… They are like beings from another, primitive world."

He raced on, as much to clarify his own reasoning as to give Ram Singh an explanation. "Bullets don't stop them—but we know that is no proof that they are demons. In your own native hills, you have seen fanatics whom a bullet would not stop, even though it pierced the heart. A charging tiger does not stop for it. In the Philippine Islands, there is a tribe of primitive men who bind their arms and legs before going into battle so as not to be weakened by loss of blood. The tribe is the Igorote. These things which we have seen tonight are possible for humans." His voice died away now.

Ram Singh sucked in a deep breath. "If they are human, I do not fear them, master. *Wah!* We are warriors, thou and I—and all humans can be killed!"

But even in his robust voice, there was a question—one that Wentworth's own mind echoed in spite of his sure logic. He swung left, at Ram Singh's direction, as they reached the outskirts of Hillville, a town, he knew, of some fifty thousand population. Presently, he turned right again. They passed no one in the deserted streets. Only the occasional dim gleam of a street light broke the darkness. In spite of himself, Wentworth flung back his head to search the skies for traces of the enemy he felt sure he had eluded. Each dark side street they passed was a threat.

"That large house on the right, two blocks ahead, master," Ram Singh directed.

Wentworth nodded and relief flooded into him. They were surely in time....

Suddenly he ripped out an oath! As he stared, he saw dark forms dart from the shrubbery about the house and converge upon it. A lance of crimson gun-flame spurted from a window and was instantly answered by an overwhelming volley from the charging men!

CHAPTER 3
THE DOCTOR'S MONKEY

INSTANTLY, WENTWORTH jammed down the accelerator, but the shattered hulk of a car already was doing its best. Swiftly, his eyes swept the scene ahead. The attackers numbered nearly a dozen men, and there might be others in concealment. Those who had answered that first gun-flash continued their ragged charge. A second shot from the window sent one reeling to the ground and the others faltered. Some flung themselves flat; others scattered left and right to circle the building.

They were no more than dim, moving shadows, but Wentworth was certain they were not the curious men-beasts. One of them had fallen at a gunshot!

"Crouch low," Wentworth snapped at Ram Singh. "Fire over their heads, unless they shoot at us—then shoot to kill. I'm going straight across the lawn up to the house!"

"Let thy servant drive, master," Ram Singh urged harshly. "No need that you...."

"Ready!" Wentworth ordered.

The car cleared the curb with a careening lurch. A tire blew out with a hissing report, but Wentworth held it steadily on its course. Ram Singh emptied an automatic in a swift drum-roll of fire. One shot answered, then the men turned and fled back into the shadows from which they had sprung and carried their wounded with them. From the house, a gun lashed out three times swiftly and another of the fugitives fell, but sprung up and raced on. His cry came to Wentworth's ears, hoarsely.

"Friends!" he shouted toward the house. "We are friends!"

He flung from the driver's seat and lifted both hands high, palms toward the house. On the other side of the car, Ram Singh followed his example.

A man's voice called suspiciously from the building, "We have no friends in this town!"

Wentworth heard a woman's tones, quick and urgent, but could not distinguish words and the man called again, grudgingly.

"You chased that mob away all right. Come on in!"

Wentworth started forward quickly.

"Keep your hands up!" the man ordered, sharply.

Wentworth quickened his stride to a run. He must make it in time now.

"Hurry, Ram Singh," he urged. "Those men may return. We'll go in by the window!"

With a quick spring, he seized the sill and muscled himself straight upward. An instant later, he was standing in the darkened room, and Ram Singh was scrambling in behind him. He could make out vaguely the outline of the man, standing with a rifle ready at his hip, and half-behind him, the slimmer, graceful outline of a girl.

"Jack!" she cried softly, "it's the fortune-teller!"

Wentworth cut in, "I'm Richard Wentworth. I came here to investigate the disappearance of some five hundred men— among them your father, Miss Rand. You *are* Miss Rand?"

The girl's assent was hurried. "Oh, if you can only find him! But I'm afraid it's too late. Those Blancos…."

"Quiet, Janet," the man cut in. "Nobody will believe that story, and there's no use…."

"I believe it," Wentworth told them quietly. "We were almost killed by a band of these… Blancos." He hesitated over the word deliberately and, while he spoke, his mind raced on. Blancos was a Spanish term for *albinos*, freaks that occasionally occurred in all species of mammals, born without pigmentation so that their bodies—even the hair—was white. But they were extraordinary. Not one in a million human beings born would show those characteristics—yet he had been attacked by no less than twelve! Moreover, the mere lack of pigmentation could never create that incredible stamina and bestiality.

"I must talk to you," Wentworth went on quietly. "Ram Singh will stand guard."

It was this quiet confidence about Wentworth which won the girl's instant trust.

"Father's laboratory is in the basement," she said quickly. "We will be safe enough in having a light there."

SHE LED the way rapidly along a dark hallway, down steep stairs at whose foot a light burned dimly. Wentworth had a glimpse there of the girl and immediately liked the proud carriage of her head, the clear frankness of her gaze as she smiled faintly back at him.

She opened a heavy metal door, and Wentworth found himself in a white, porcelain-fitted room which he recognized instantly as a biological laboratory. One wall was filled with cages and in one a large white ape set up a chattering challenge. One bent arm shielded its eyes with a gesture curiously human. The animal was an albino! But what connection could there be between this white, imprisoned monkey and those other bestial Blancos that had attacked him?

"This is my fiancé, Jack Dawson," the girl said quietly, and Wentworth turned to confront the man. He was twenty-two or three with determination in the long, set line of his jaw; shrewd calculation showed in the spaced, grey eyes.

Wentworth thrust out his hand in a spontaneous gesture of approval and, after a grudging moment, the man gripped it hard.

"You'll have to pardon my belligerence," Dawson said gravely, "but the town seems to have gone crazy. Those men intended to lynch us both! They still seem to blame us for the… disappearance of Janet's father."

"Miss Rand—"

Wentworth swung to her—"your father has been experimenting with albinos?"

Janet's eyes met his squarely. Her thick braids of honey-colored hair, twined in a coronet, made her head seem too heavy for its slender throat—a suggestion that reminded Wentworth achingly of his own love in far-away New York, Nita van Sloan.

"Yes," Janet Rand answered his question clearly, "but if you blame him…."

Wentworth brushed the suggestion aside, more a tribute to her loyalty than a decision on Dr. Rand's possible guilt.

"I'm not blaming him," he said, "but Doctor Rand was the only one of the five hundred or more who have disappeared who might be termed an educated man. I believe that fact has some significance. It is why I came to you. Can you suggest anything? Has any friend of your father been especially interested in his experiments? Have there been any inquiries…?"

Jack Dawson exclaimed sharply, "Hans Lieberling!"

"That's silly," Janet insisted hotly. "You're just jealous of him, Jack!"

Wentworth stood quietly studying the two, saw the swift flush that reddened Dawson's face.

Janet swung toward Wentworth. "Dr. Lieberling is an ethnologist also," she said, "or rather an anthropologist. He's been after Dad for two months to take him as an associate. But Dad wanted exclusive credit for his work...."

Wentworth frowned and crossed toward the ape, which had ceased its chattering, but still protected its eyes behind a baby-like hand. In the shadow, the eyes showed pink. Wentworth held out a hand to the ape, and it reached out to grasp his fingers, as confidingly as a child. Wentworth's eyes shifted to the other inmates of the cages, rats, guinea pigs, rabbits—*and all of them albinos!*

"Lieberling is here in town?" he asked.

"At the Hill House," Janet answered.

"Was this ape born an albino?" Wentworth dropped the question casually, but as he turned, he was aware of an abrupt stiffening in Janet Rand's mien.

"I really can't see, Mr. Wentworth," she said, "that the fact has any connection with my father's disappearance!"

Wentworth nodded absently, but his mind leaped to the obvious conclusion that Rand had been experimenting with artificially created albinos—and five hundred men had disappeared!

The furious pounding of feet upon the steep stairs jerked all three toward the door, which batted open to show the fierce face of Ram Singh.

"Master!" he gasped. "Master, I have heard the hunting cry of the demons!"

WITH AN oath, Wentworth sprang toward the door, heard the others crowd through the narrow passage in his wake as he took the stairs with leaping strides. Ram Singh was right behind him, and in the narrow hallway above, Wentworth rasped out a few quick words in Punjabi.

"In the basement is a white ape," he said. "Get it and bring it to your room at the Hill House!"

"*Han, sahib,*" Ram Singh muttered and gave the room number. "But these demons—"

"They will undoubtedly come here," Wentworth snapped. "I'll have to get these people away. After that, I do not know."

In the dark room he had first entered, Wentworth paused to listen. Once again, through the still darkness of the night, he heard that rising, hideous scream. It was ominously near. Wentworth whirled, as Dawson and Janet Rand entered behind him.

"The Blancos will come here for you," he said curtly. "Bullets will not stop them. The best thing you can do is to leave town by the main highway north, and go fast."

Blank silence greeted him and Dawson's voice, when he spoke, was hoarse. "What do you mean—bullets will not stop them?"

"I have no time for argument," Wentworth snapped, and the accent of command was in his voice—the voice of a true master of men! "If you wish, you may come with me! I must do what I can to organize a defense!"

As he spoke, he was striding toward the door. He heard Dawson and the girl in swift debate, then their feet came rapidly after him.

"My car is at the curb," Dawson said. "We'll stick with you!"

Wentworth did not check his pounding stride toward the car, but his heart warmed at their decision. More than trust—it

30

was a pledge of comradeship. Accustomed though he was to winning these
prompt loyalties, he could not keep the
smile from his lips. This was the only
reward he had, or sought, for his ceaseless and selfless battle against death
and crime—that now and again the
hearts of the people went out to him.

It was as if they could recognize under the set, often stern, exte-
rior, the warmth of his altruism.

"I think," he said quietly, as the car leaped forward under
Dawson's expert hands, "that you can serve best by fleeing from
Hillville. Go to Franklin and find lodging. Let me know where
to find you. It's very clear that something you know is of vital
importance to the criminals. If you could tell me what that is—"

"But we don't know!" Janet cried. "I've been trying hard to
think what it could be. I don't know. Father's experiments were
concerned with artificially creating albinos, but I know nothing
at all about it." She broke off abruptly, then, "We left the fortune
teller behind!" she cried.

"He has his orders," Wentworth said curtly. "Will you take
me to the Hill House, then get out of town?"

"It's running away!" Dawson said doggedly. "They'll blame us
more than ever about the doctor. God knows I never wish him
any harm! I didn't think he was quite fair to Janet...."

"You didn't know, Jack!"

"Also, he was opposed to us getting married," Dawson went

on. "But it wasn't anything serious. I'd give my right hand to get him back safely!"

"If you stay, Janet will stay," Wentworth said quietly, "and I doubt if either of you would worry long about what people thought of you."

"What do you mean?" Dawson demanded harshly.

Wentworth said gently, "You'd be dead!"

In the shaken silence afterward, Dawson whirled a corner sharply and, from between two darkened houses, a huge white figure shambled forward at a bestial run, charging for the car. Dawson swore and trod the accelerator. They roared past and, looking back, Wentworth saw the Blanco take then trail at a trot.

Dawson's profile was set in harsh lines. "I'm not afraid," he said flatly, "but I can't let anything happen to Janet!"

Janet started a protest, but Wentworth laid a hand on her arm, and she fell silent. His appeal had been instinctive.

"We'll go," she assented.

Wentworth made no reply, but sent his sharp glance probing ahead through the night, as they raced for the downtown district of Hillville. The Blanco who had stumbled on their trail was undoubtedly an accident, but his presence meant that there must be many of his kind scattered through the town. The thought was ominous. Men whom not even bullets could stop would be able to sack the city....

Wentworth shook his head irritably. The Blancos would not have the intelligence for that. Men of that primitive stamina were necessarily of low mental order. It was not the Blancos, but the men behind them that were most to be feared! Criminals who would release such a slaughtering horror upon the world, were more beasts than men—but *intelligent* beasts! A fresh realization crashed upon his thoughts. Such an attack as the presence of the Blancos indicated had not been launched solely to exterminate Janet Rand and her sweetheart. Something much more far-reaching was intended. Good God, could they mean to sack the city!

"Police headquarters," he snapped at Dawson, "then fly for your lives! The best your car will do won't be fast enough!"

Dawson's white face jerked toward him an instant, then swung back, and the roar of the engine deepened. Wentworth was conscious of Janet's hand gripping his arm.

"Mr. Wentworth," she said slowly, "it seems selfish at a time like this to think of father, but if—if you can find him…."

"I will," Wentworth told her shortly. "I have a plan."

The car stopped with a screech of locked tires before the twin green lamps of the police headquarters, and Wentworth leaped to the pavement.

"Hurry," he directed shortly. "I'll be at the Hill House." He did not add that, if his fears were well founded, even the Hill House might not be there on the morrow! With a wave of his hand, he went bounding up the steps into the station.

BEHIND THE desk, the night sergeant nodded sleepily, but his head snapped up at the sight of Wentworth, and the sound of his urgent voice. "Get hold of the police chief at once," Wentworth directed. "An army of criminals is marching on the city!"

The sergeant narrowed his eyes, "Listen, buddy," he said dryly, "it would be worth my job to call the chief at this time of night.

An army of criminals… Say, what brand of mountain dew have you been drinking?"

Impatience goaded Wentworth cruelly, but he held his temper in check. Command crackled in his voice now. "Obey, Sergeant," he snapped.

The man's head jerked up, and doubt crept into his eyes as they met the piercing, fierce regard of Richard Wentworth. He suddenly crumbled.

"All right," he temporized, "I'll call him, but if he's sore…" His voice trailed off, and he picked up the telephone.

As soon as he had given the number, Wentworth snatched the instrument from his hands. "Get the local commander of the national guard on the phone," he directed. "I'll talk to the chief."

Wentworth's vibrant force galvanized the slow-minded sergeant. He recognized authority when he heard it. Wentworth ignored him while the chief's sleepy, voice grumbled in his ear.

"Major Wentworth, national guard, speaking," Wentworth used a legitimate title, but one without force in Kentucky. "There's a band of criminals moving in on Hillville right now. I'm mobilizing the national guard, but we won't be quick enough. Do you have grenades in your equipment?"

The chief echoed vacantly, "Grenades? Why, I think we've got a part of a case…."

"Chief," Wentworth cut in savagely, "this is life and death! There will be dozens of people killed here tonight if you don't snap out of your lethargy and get busy. I'd hate to report to the governor…."

There was a crashing rattle on the wire, and the sergeant's voice cut in hurriedly.

"Hey, Chief… Sergeant Morgan. I thought this guy was nuts, but I just got a phone call from Jess Franklin up on Elm Street and he says a mob of white giants—that's what he called them— crashed into the house next door. He saw old Mrs. Mercer torn to pieces and that daughter of hers… God, it was awful! Jess says he shot three of them through the heart and they turned around and came after him. He ran like hell. He says there's dozens of them, and…."

"I'll be right down," the chief said fumblingly. "Major, if you could help, I… Good God, there's something climbing up on the porch roof! Oh, my God!"

A crash of glass sounded, a distant thud that Wentworth knew must be a gun firing, and after that there were only screams—the cry of a man in awful fear and greater pain, and of a beast, triumphant!

CHAPTER 4
THE DEMONS DANCE

WENTWORTH HUNG up crisply, horror tightening his eyes and bringing anger pumping through his veins. But the death of one man—and he had no doubt of the chief's death—must not slow the defense of the city. Wentworth swung on Sergeant Morgan, who came crashing back into the office.

"We got to get to the chief!" Morgan shouted. "We gotta…."

"The chief is dead," Wentworth said coldly. "You cannot help him. You heard the chief tell me to take charge, Sergeant—you were on the wire. Here are your orders!"

While Morgan stared at him haggardly Wentworth drummed precise instructions, though he could see the words only bounced from the man's horror-struck mind. Suddenly, the sergeant's horror broke out in furious rage.

"By God, we'll wipe them out!" he shouted. "I'll get the boys...."

"You'll obey orders, Sergeant Morgan!" Wentworth snapped. "Your men wouldn't last two minutes against this kind of set-up. Didn't you hear Jess Franklin say even heart shots didn't stop them? He told the truth. We have only one hope—grenades and dynamite."

Morgan faced him, white-faced. "Not even heart shots," he whispered.

Fiercely, Wentworth threw orders at him. "Find and break out the grenades; smash open whatever explosives store there was in the city and bring the supplies to headquarters. Send the squad car with grenades to Elm Street. They are to throw the grenades, then race back to headquarters," Wentworth hurried on. "If they attempt to fight with guns, they'll be butchered!"

The hammer of Wentworth's commanding voice broke through Morgan's daze. He snapped out, "Yes, sir," turned and ran back through the broad hallway. Wentworth sprang to the telephone.

"Call out all reserves," he directed the operator. "Extreme emergency. Men to rush to headquarters with all speed.

Commandeer all automobiles on the way and bring them here!… Get me the commander of the national guard here, also."

It was ten minutes before the squad car got away with the grenades, another five before men set off toward the explosive depot. By that time, Wentworth had found out the local guard commander, Major Charles Hascomb, was out of the city; had contacted the second in command, one Captain Carstairs. Carstairs refused to act in the absence of orders. He doubted that Major Hascomb was out of the city since he had had no word of his superior's absence.

"Very well," Wentworth said, furiously cold, "I will give the orders. I am your senior and you should know enough to remember that, in time of emergency, the senior officer commands regardless of jurisdiction. You will call out your men at once, arm them with grenades and report to me at police headquarters without delay. Commandeer cars. This is extreme emergency."

Captain Carstairs hesitated, then said crisply, "Yes, sir. At once, sir—on your responsibility."

"On my responsibility," Wentworth bit out. He choked back the bitter laughter that surged to his lips. At a time like this, men could think of *responsibility!* Call after call was crashing into the police headquarters, frantic cries for help, reports of ghastly crimes. Those reports came from widely scattered sections of the city. Plainly, there were a half dozen mobs of those damnable Blancos at their work of murder and destruction!

WENTWORTH HAD to hold tightly to himself to keep from dashing to the battle, but he realized that here, at headquarters, he could be many times more effective than in single combat. He organized men to convert the sticks of commandeered dynamite into short-fused bombs; sent cars of police, armed with them, to whatever point was threatened. But the squad car—the first to leave—had not returned. Wentworth

One Blanco was hurled bodily in the
air as the grenade went off!

swore under his breath. Had the fools tried to fight with guns
in spite of his instructions?

In the street, a siren made a low, whimpering moan, like an

animal in pain, and there was a rending, shattering crash that jarred the very walls of headquarters! Wentworth dashed to the door—and stood motionless while fear gripped his heart—his fear not for himself, but the city's thousands. The squad car had come back and it was evident that not even grenades would stop the Blancos!

The squad car was jammed, its radiator crumpled, against the front of headquarters, a wreck—but it was not the collision that had done it. The sides were ripped from it, fenders and tires hacked to fragments. Of the ten men who had gone forth, only one had returned. He lay, a broken and bleeding thing, across the steering-wheel. This was the challenge.

"Get that man inside," Wentworth ordered. "See if you can learn from him what the grenades accomplished."

Four white-faced police went tremblingly forward to get their comrade. Wentworth sent another to call for an ambulance or a doctor. Around the corner of the street, a column of men swung at double-time, carrying rifles, canvas grenade bags at their hips. Wentworth's eyes ran keenly over the line, took in their commanding officer at a glance. They seemed well disciplined, but they would confront an enemy that might well shatter the morale of veteran troops—an enemy whom they could not stop with either their rifles nor the bayonets they had been taught to believe invincible! But they swung into a swift company-front, and Captain Carstairs came striding toward headquarters. It was a tribute to Wentworth's commanding presence that he walked directly to him, saluting.

"Captain Carstairs reporting, sir," he said, "with Company B."

"How many more men have you, Captain?"

"Three more companies, sir," Carstairs reported, while his eyes probed Wentworth's. "They will report here as fast as formed."

Wentworth nodded, drew Carstairs inside headquarters where he made a swift summary of the situation. He could see incredulity grow in the man's eyes, but fought down his impatience.

"Did you notice the squad car out front?" he asked quietly. "That went out with ten men, armed with grenades. Their opponents carried only knives."

Carstairs' face paled. "If grenades can't stop them…."

Wentworth waved a hand impatiently. "I don't know how efficiently the grenades were used, or whether the police disobeyed orders and tried to use their pistols afterward. Here are your orders, Captain. You will take command here, resisting any attempt of civil authorities to supersede you, pending orders from the capital.

"As your companies report, you will hold two platoons in reserve here. The others you will dispatch to danger points as reported. I shall mount this company in automobiles and make a swift circuit of outlying districts, attempt to establish contact. When I have discovered a way to fight these Blancos, I will phone orders to you. Until that time, your orders are that the men will throw grenades and retreat promptly."

"Retreat, sir?" Carstairs stammered.

"Retreat and fight a rear-guard action," Wentworth said curtly. "On no account are they to allow the enemy to come to grips. By repeated grenade attacks, and retreats, you should be

41

able to destroy the enemy. If they come to grips, your men will be wiped out instantly. You understand your instructions fully, Captain?"

Captain Carstairs' voice was taut, "Yes, sir."

Wentworth nodded and strode out to the company. Briefly, he repeated the gist of his instructions for battle contact.

"You will work in half-squads in separate cars," he concluded. "I will hold each non-commissioned officer personally accountable if he allows his men to come to grips with the enemy. Officers, distribute your men! Fall out!"

They obeyed.

WITHIN LESS than ten minutes after the national guard unit had reported, Wentworth had his automobile troop under way. A second company swung into the street before headquarters as they raced off on their circuit of the city.

Far away against the southeastern skyline, fire glow was red against the sky. There was another blaze off to the south. But for the most part, the town of Hillville was dark, its thousands sleeping in ignorance of the nightmarish peril at their doors. It was better so, Wentworth believed. Panic would only simplify the work of murder and rapine loosed upon the town.

Twice in the first dozen blocks, automobiles scuttled across Wentworth's path like frightened animals, carrying overloads of frightened people. Wentworth pushed on. He had a double purpose in circling the town. He wanted to locate the line of retreat of the Blancos and cut them off; or, if they still poured into Hillville, he must smash them back into the hills from which they undoubtedly came.

42

Wentworth, in the lead, had covered the better part of two miles before he heard again the awful, challenging scream of the Blancos. It reached his ears, faintly. Beside him, on the front seat, the young driver of the car stirred uneasily. Wentworth glanced at him fully, looked back at the three other men in the rear. Their faces were grimly set. The scream came again, fierce in the darkness.

"Stop here," Wentworth ordered curtly. He picked out one of the men in the rear. "Tell the cars behind to turn and face the other way, two abreast. At a signal of two pistol shots from me, or other sign, they are to roll, fast enough to keep ahead of the Blancos. Grenades, when they are near enough. Rifles, until then. They are to shoot for the legs. You will stay with the last car you notify."

The man scrambled out and jogged back with the grenade bag thudding against his hip. Wentworth turned to the driver.

"When I order to turn, do it in one loop if you have to crash through a tree to do it. Understand?"

The driver nodded silently, eyes straight ahead. He was like a machine.

"All right," Wentworth directed. "When we sight the Blancos, you will open rifle fire on command. Shoot for the legs. When they are close enough, we will throw grenades—on command. Immediately afterward, we will retreat. Go ahead, driver. Turn to the right at this corner!"

Wentworth felt his breath crowd gustily into his throat. Would his combat plan work—or would there be another wrecked car with its cargo of dead and dying? The car rolled rapidly forward, took the corner heeling. Wentworth's eyes searched the darkness ahead. Lights were beginning to spring up in houses. A window was flung wide, and a man leaped out, peering—a woman crowding behind him.

And then Wentworth heard the cries—this time not the screams of Blancos, but of women. The screams tore out, hoarse, terror-laden—then broke off sharply.

"Turn left," Wentworth directed quietly.

Perspiration beaded the forehead of the driver. His hands were bone-white upon the wheel, and Wentworth remembered that these men had homes here—perhaps in this immediate neighborhood. A block further on, they spotted the first faint flickerings of flame against the side of a building.

"Halt!" Wentworth snapped.

He peered into the shadows, and suddenly those shadows erupted giant white figures, charging forward, leaping high, screaming, and brandishing their fierce knives!

"Grenades!" Wentworth snapped. "Throw them in their path!"

Behind, he caught the curses of the men. He threw up his automatic and broke a leg on the first of the Blancos. The fire was leaping up the building wall now and, against that lurid glare, the figures of the beast-men were plainly outlined. He saw two grenades, black balls wobbling through the glare toward the on-rushing horde.

"Turn!" he snapped at the driver.

The car leaped forward, cut sharply about, bounded over the

curb and trundled for fifty feet along the sidewalk before it lurched back to the street.

BEHIND THEM, the grenades let go almost at the same instant. A scrap of torn metal slammed tinnily into the back of the car. Twisted around in his seat, Wentworth saw a Blanco hurled bodily into the air—beheld another go down with his legs blown nearly from his body. Three others staggered, fell but were up instantly, charging forward at furious speed. The automobile picked up momentum.

"Slowly," Wentworth warned the driver, "now rifle fire. Aim, hold and squeeze—*at their legs!*"

Some of the Blancos sprinted along the pavement in the shadows of the trees. Others pounded down the middle of the street—and the three whom the grenade fragments had torn ran more swiftly than the others! The rifles began to crack. All about them, from the houses that were springing to life, came screams and hoarse shouts. One Blanco went down with a rifle-broken leg, scrambled up and began to hop forward again to the attack.

The swearing of the rifle-men was high, thin—almost hysterical.

"You can't stop them!" one cried. "I broke his leg, and…."

"Break the other," Wentworth ordered calmly.

The man twisted and stared at Wentworth, and on Wentworth's lips was a calm smile.

The man laughed inanely. "Why, sure!" he gasped. "Why, sure—now I break the other one!"

Presently, the Blanco went down just before the car turned the first corner, and the last glimpse Wentworth had of the creature, it was dragging itself forward on great arms, lips open in a challenging scream! The Blancos were now rapidly closing the gap between them and the slowly rolling car.

"Grenades," Wentworth snapped again. "One each. Throw in their path!"

And then he saw it—a fresh swarm of Blancos burst from between two houses a hundred feet ahead of them. The driver saw it at the same instant and, instinctively, stepped down on the throttle.

"Turn!" Wentworth snapped.

Behind them, the grenades cut loose deafeningly and screams that seemed to tear the very skies rolled out of that geyser of flame and destruction. The car heeled far over, tires shrieking, as the driver obeyed Wentworth's command.

"Full speed!" Wentworth barked. "Grenades, one each," he hurled at the men behind.

His automatic was in his hand. Ahead now were the remnants of the pursuing band of Blancos. The first group had been caught in the double concussion of the grenades and torn apart, but ten of the creatures still were on their feet and racing toward the car. A grenade erupted just before them, but one man caught almost the full force of the blast. It tore him apart. One other went down, legs shattered by flying fragments, but the others raced on and the second grenade was late—blasting behind them.

"Rifles!" Wentworth called.

One of the Blancos was charging straight toward them along the street, head-on for the car.

"Hit him!" Wentworth ordered quietly.

His automatic began to kick in his hand. He fired directly through the windshield, and the punched holes the bullets made kept tally on his shots. He knocked one of the Blancos off his feet, threw lead at a second and missed. Too late now for grenades. They would do more damage to the car and to its occupants than to the Blancos.

The driver was swearing between tight lips, trying to jockey a few miles more speed out of the car. At the instant when they were about to ram the charging Blanco, the beast-man leaped high into the air! His feet almost cleared the radiator. It struck his ankles, whipped his heavy body down full force across the windshield. His head crunched on the top and the blade of his knife sliced down through the metal, and caught the driver.

Alongside Wentworth, the driver screamed horribly. His death-contorted body tried to rear upward, but the knife had driven down into his skull and held him there. Wentworth grabbed for the wheel—too late. Careening wildly, the car leaped the curb, crashed through a low hedge and slammed against the porch of a house.

"Grenades!" Wentworth shouted. "Get into the house!"

He leaped to the ground, hurdled the steps in a single leap. The thunder of the grenades seemed to beat against him with physical force, then the two panting men were scrambling up the steps beside him. Wentworth lashed out with his gun and smashed the glass from the front door, reached through to open it.

"Drop a grenade here," he ordered, "and follow me!"

Straight through the hall they hammered and out the back

door. A garage stood in the back yard, but its doors were locked and there was no likelihood that the keys would be in the car.

"Run at top speed!" Wentworth snapped. "You, leave your rifle and grenades. Get back to the cars and send them here. They are to duplicate our tactics. Grenades, retreat. The Blancos will follow and they may be able to destroy them! Run, damn you!"

He faced the other man. "Our first stand is behind the garage." THE MAN nodded and ran heavily beside him, loaded with rifle and grenades. His face was dead white, almost luminous in the darkness. The shattering crash of the grenade left in the front doorway had died amid screams and the howls of the Blancos came from within the house. At the instant they reached the garage, Wentworth peered back and saw lights blaze out in the upper story. A woman ran across a room and caught up a baby from its crib. Wentworth groaned.

"This way!" he shouted through cupped hands. "Out the back window to the porch roof!"

The woman either did not hear or was too frightened to heed. She ran out of the doorway into the darkness of the hall beyond. With an oath, Wentworth ran forward.

"Hide!" he ordered the man behind him. "They won't be apt to find you here!"

He was already halfway to the house, as he finished. A leap took him to the porch, to the railing. An upward jump and he had hold of the eaves, muscled himself to the tin roof of the back porch. He scrambled across, climbed in through the window.

"This way!" he shouted—and heard the woman scream, heard the thin, coughing wail of a young baby.

To the door, Wentworth leaped. A Blanco had reached the head of the stairs. Wentworth's gun convulsed in his hand, and the creature's right leg punched backward, but his grip on the railing held him erect.

"This way," Wentworth called calmly to the woman.

She squeezed past the out-reaching hands of the Blancos as Wentworth fired again. The beast-man's face was twisted into bestial lines. It lunged forward and broken legs collapsed beneath it. But it advanced crawling on hands and broken stumps. Wentworth smashed a bullet through the head that tore off half the skull and still, for four yards, the creature came on until the bloody, dying thing was within a foot of where he stood. Wentworth sprang through the doorway and there, the Blanco died. Wentworth yanked the pin of a grenade and hurled it down the stairway, sprang toward the woman.

"Out the window," he ordered. "There's just a chance…."

He started across the tin roof toward the edge, and a swarm of Blancos swirled around the house. One of them saw him and raised the shrill hunting cry. Wentworth fired straight into the beast-thing's face, saw it hurled to the ground. Instantly, the Blanco was up. With two long bounds, it reached the porch. There was a straining, creaking sound of breaking wood, and the Blanco ripped a corner column out from beneath the roof! It sagged drunkenly, and Wentworth retreated toward the house.

Swiftly, he lobbed another grenade down among the gathered Blancos, and, as he did so, realized there were only two more grenades in his pouch. Behind him, the woman screamed terribly. He whirled in time to see the hands of a Blanco snatch the baby from her arms!

CHAPTER 5
QUEST OF THE APE

WENTWORTH HAD only one chance to smash the Blanco's arms with bullets while they were still extended for the baby. The mother was rushing forward to the attack in frantic forgetfulness of her own danger, and, with each passing instant, the passage through which he must hurl his lead was narrowing. He threw two shots that sounded almost as one, and for a blurred instant could not be sure what had happened.

The mother dropped to her knees, and the Blanco's scream rose hoarsely. Even as Wentworth realized that his lead had at least forced the beast to drop the baby, the Blanco charged into the room. One broken, lashing arm struck the mother and hurled her against the wall with her baby, then the creature rushed for the window where Wentworth crouched.

Beneath his feet, the roof was sagging as another post wrenched from its foundations. His grenades were useless and the gun... He fired three shots in rapid succession, two to the legs, one to the head—and still the beast, whipping bloody foam from its lips, came on. Behind him, Wentworth heard a grenade's thunder, and shrill screams—heard a man's cry.

He wrenched about and saw that two of the Blancos were climbing toward him. From beside the garage, rifle flame was spurting as the soldier entered the battle. Some of the Blancos whirled that way. One went down, a grenade blew two others almost to bits, but the others rushed on—four still on their feet. Wentworth emptied his automatic in a swift effort to avert the inevitable. One of the Blancos fell with a shattered spine, but the others reached the soldier. He screamed only once.

Braced against the house, Wentworth waited his own doom. Grenades would be useless against the two creatures mounting to his now precarious perch. The dying Blanco in the window could not reach him, but still blocked the way to retreat. With feverish hands, Wentworth reloaded his automatic. He pumped three bullets into the first head that showed itself, then whirled toward the window. He seized the dying beast by a broken arm and threw all his strength into a heave.

Teeth fastened in Wentworth's hand, but he did not release his hold. There was no time for another. He heaved again, and the Blanco lunged toward him. Wentworth pivoted on a heel, released his grip and the heavy body struck the roof-top, tumbled screaming toward where its mates clambered upward.

There was a tremendous creaking of the timbers, and Wentworth seized the sides of the window, jerked himself inside just in time. The porch roof collapsed, and carrying the Blancos with it. An instant later, he heard the heavy blasts of grenades in the street, the shrill rallying screams of the Blancos. Wentworth turned heavily from the window, found the woman crouched, whimpering, over her child. She stared up at him, the madness of terror in her eyes.

Wentworth moved into the hallway. She was probably safer here than elsewhere, since the soldiers had arrived to battle the

In his last half-conscious moment, he heard
Nita's despairing cry, "Save yourself, Dick!"

Blancos. There would be casualties, but in the main the strategy
he had arranged would be successful. He stumbled down the

steps, found a telephone and called police headquarters. He was put through instantly to Carstairs.

"Grenades stop the Blancos to an extent," Wentworth told him swiftly, and described the method he had devised. "We are engaged with nearly fifty of the Blancos and have killed many of them. Two of our men are dead. No, I don't know their names."

He listened intently then while Carstairs rattled off details of other attacks, one of them in the downtown district where soldiers had been beaten off with heavy losses.

"They've blown the vaults in our three banks," Carstairs rushed on, "and I'm helpless to stop them. I'm putting men on rooftops with our one machine gun."

"Good," Wentworth snapped. "Carry on."

HE LEFT the phone, crept toward the front door. The battle had withdrawn down the street where a mob of Blancos was pursuing slowly retreating automobiles. Now and again, another of the white monsters would fall. Wentworth sprang to the car, lodged against the steps of the house. It was sickening work to dislodge the Blanco from its roof and free the knife from the soldier it had killed, but Wentworth managed it.

Five minutes later, he was roaring down the street—away from the scene of battle and toward the place where the attack on the banks raged. His work here was done—the soldiers could carry on the fight now that he had shown them the way. The work of the Spider lay ahead. Down there, where the banks were being looted, he would find the criminals behind these atrocities, if he were in time....

Wentworth raced to the Hill House. With the heavy roll of

nearby gunfire in his ears, he was forced to climb to a second-floor window to enter because of barricaded doors, but finally he reached Ram Singh's room. Obedient to orders, the Sikh was there with the white ape. There was a bloody gash across Ram Singh's bearded cheek and one arm was wound with a crude bandage.

"Tie up the ape," Wentworth snapped. "There is work!"

He whipped a suitcase, part of Ram Singh's luggage, from beneath the bed and spread it open on the bureau. It revealed a complete make-up kit, and Wentworth's hands flew over the familiar contents. A lotion, rapidly patted on, tautened the skin of his face until it stretched tightly across the cheekbones, turned sallow. Rapidly, he altered the shape of his nose until it was hawk-like, predatory. His mouth became a lipless gash and bushy eyebrows covered his own. Then he drew over his head a wig of lank hair and it was no longer Richard Wentworth, wealthy clubman and dilettante of the arts and criminology, that peered back at him from the mirror. It was the dread face of the man whom criminals feared more than all the minions or the law—of the Spider!

A wide-brimmed black hat, a black cape snatched from the suitcase and Wentworth was now ready for the foray.

"Death can't stop these Blancos," he said hurriedly, "but fear may. Primitive minds are all superstitious."

Ram Singh's bearded lips moved in a slight smile. "Death can stop them, master!" he said.

Wentworth felt a smile touch his lips, the first that he had

55

known since this horror struck the city. So simply, Ram Singh chronicled what must have been heroic battle!

"Thou art brave, my warrior," he said softly. "Now this is my plan. Fortunately, this is one of my new capes—fireproofed. I shall dip parts of it in gasoline and charge the Blancos."

"Master!" Ram Singh cried.

Wentworth moved a hand impatiently. "Listen," he said shortly. Into the silence that fell between them, the heavy hammer of the guns rolled, the screams of the beast-men and the more awful screams of their victims.

"Come," Wentworth said softly. "You will cover me with gunfire when possible. Don't count on killing the Blancos— shoot for their legs and arms."

HE LED the way swiftly along the deserted hotel corridor down a fire-escape. Minutes later, he had doused the outside of the cape in gasoline and was rushing toward the sounds of battle. The cape had been intended only as a protection against fire and the flames would run up toward his head, but if he moved swiftly....

At the corner of Main Street, Wentworth paused and peered around at the bank halfway down the block. Over the street ranged a dozen Blancos. Only dead men opposed them, but the Blancos were not content with that. They beat and hacked at corpses. As Wentworth looked, the machine gun which had kept up a yammer from above stopped suddenly. There was a combined, rising shriek, Blanco and terrified human together, and a body in soldier's uniform crashed down into the street.

At the doors of the bank, Blancos moved hurriedly in and out, loading money-stuffed bags into a car.

"Keep to cover," Wentworth snapped at Ram Singh. "You can serve me best with the guns!"

He stooped and struck a match to the gasoline and, instantly, sprinted into the open. He felt the hot lash of the first fumes igniting, then the light of the flames leaped ahead of him. His cape tugged and flapped at his shoulders with the speed of his running and the crackle and dull roar of the wind-fanned fire dinned in his ears. With his first bound, Wentworth parted his lips and uttered a weird, wailing scream—such a scream as the East knew and had come to fear. It was the cry of the murderous dacoits. Wentworth used it to terrify. He was a burning man, a weird and ominous figure who ran with the flames and screamed like a beast of the wilds.

Instantly, every Blanco eye was turned toward him. A man at the doorway of the bank crouched half behind a pillar and opened fire, but Ram Singh's ready guns answered and Wentworth saw that, strangely, this Blanco could not resist the hammer of lead. He fell kicking, screaming, to the ground!

"Run!" Wentworth shouted. "Run, fools! Blancos! The wraths of the jungle gods is loose. The gods are angry. I will burn you—burn you!"

A wavering moan of terror wailed from the Blancos. One huge fellow stood in Wentworth's path, empty-handed, great arms swinging in mounting anger. Wentworth raced directly at him, unswerving, darting straight into the face of death—if fear failed to shake the man from his stand. He reached back a hand and gripped the inside of his cape. Abruptly, the Blanco charged!

Wentworth ran straight at him, pivoted on a heel and flung the burning side of the cape against the Blanco's face! The Blanco screamed in tortured pain, whirled and fled, and the impact of his terror-stricken panic propelled the others into stampede. In an instant, they were fleeing. The automobile before the bank lurched forward, and Ram Singh's bullets slammed tinnily into its back. Wentworth's own guns leaped to his hands, but the car whirled and was gone.

To the door of the bank, Wentworth darted. He could not stop, lest the flames injure him and it would be minutes before they died. Into the bank, he plunged… and found it was empty save for the dead.

Wentworth cursed in disappointment, slipped the cape from his shoulders and smothered the remaining flames by folding the cape in upon itself. It was not enough for him that he had smashed the heart of the Blanco attack. He had hoped to find the leaders of the Blanco pack here and destroy them. He ran back to the door. The Blanco Ram Singh had shot down lay dead upon the threshold and Wentworth saw that Ram Singh's bullet had snapped his neck.

With his lips thinning bitterly, Wentworth stooped beside the man and, thumbing off the base of his cigarette lighter, ground it against the dead forehead. At least the enemy should know that he had entered the battle. When they saw his seal here, they would know a remorseless foe was on their trail, a nemesis whom only death could stop. He stood, glaring down at the dead man, and on that bestial forehead was a scarlet stain like blood—a stain that had the hairy, sprawled legs, the poison fangs of the Spider! He ran toward Ram Singh.

"Back to the hotel room and get the ape," he ordered. "Bring some writing paper and a pencil. I'll get a car and meet you at the side door."

WHEN RAM SINGH returned with the ape on his shoulder, Wentworth ordered a course toward the southeastern limits of the city.

"The Blancos struck there first," he said rapidly, "and the chances are they came from that direction in the hills."

While the ape huddled, frightened, in his arms, Wentworth scrawled a note with the materials Ram Singh had brought and fastened it to the ape's collar. Swiftly, he outlined his plan. "This ape is obviously a pet," he said. "If we can release it anywhere in the vicinity in which Doctor Rand is at present, I think it may lead us to him."

Ram Singh's eyes narrowed. "My master believes the *hakim* is the pack leader of the beasts?"

Wentworth shrugged. He was far from sure what he believed, but that was the one trail open to investigation and at least he knew that Rand was with the Blancos, though it might be as a prisoner.

"Fastened to the ape's collar," Wentworth explained, "is a note giving an address in Franklin where Janet Rand and Dawson can be found. It is false, of course. I do not know where they are. But if the trail tonight fails, we still may watch that address.

The leaders of the Blancos would believe the girl was trying to communicate with her father… *Good God, Ram Singh, look!"*

From a side street surged a horde of the Blancos, but they were not roaming at large as were the others. In the glare of the headlights, it was plain that a leash was fastened to the neck of each and behind, holding the chains that bound them, was another, larger Blanco who whirled a huge, long-lashed whip about his head. The tip of the lash caught flashes of light like a jewel. It was steel-tipped!

Even as Wentworth stared, the whip lashed out, and the man uttered a peculiar, high-pitched call! The Blancos whirled—and lifted rifles to their shoulders! Ram Singh waited for no orders. With a lightning twist on the wheel, he whirled the car out of the street, crashing through a hedge and onto the lawn of a house. Without slowing, he slanted between two houses, rammed and smashed through a light wooden fence and was racing through into the next street.

It was neatly executed and swiftly. Within seconds, they were roaring on to the south along a parallel street and the rifle squad of Blancos was left behind.

"**GOOD WORK,** Ram Singh," Wentworth said slowly but he was lost in frowning concentration. The Blancos were deadly enough, with their murderous knives, but if they had been trained to use rifles, they were an incredible menace. They would not have the intelligence to find range or determine windage—even to set the sights once those were known. But if someone were to make these adjustments for them, they would be deadly marksmen.

Wentworth had personal knowledge of a team of Haitian marksmen—men of such low mentality that they even forgot their names from one day to the next, but who had been trained by United States Marines. They had beat their trainers in marksmanship! Stolidity and absolute absence of nervousness was their asset.

"Master," Ram Singh interrupted hesitantly, "there was a man at Hill House who often had gone to the home of Rand *hakim.*"

"Hans Lieberling?" Wentworth asked swiftly.

"Some such name, master," Ram Singh agreed. "When the Blancos were attacking, I saw him watch them through glasses from his window and, after a while, he walked out into the street and went among them and was not harmed."

"The devil, he did!" Wentworth muttered. "Thank you, Ram Singh. It is possible that he and not Rand..." He broke off. He could not pursue that line of investigation now. He had another more important task ahead.

"When we reach the environs of the city," Wentworth said quietly, "you will carry on alone. I must get word to the governor and have him declare martial law throughout this area. I can only hope that the operations of these criminals are isolated here. If they are widespread..." Wentworth's voice trailed off.

"There is an airport on the northern boundary of the city, *sahib,*" Ram Singh assented gravely.

Wentworth nodded. "Under no circumstances, Ram Singh," he directed, "are you to join battle with these Blancos. Your job is to follow the ape, if possible—otherwise, to trail retreating parties of the Blancos and find their hiding-place. Report afterward to me at Hill House. I suspect that the Blancos have a keenly developed sense of smell so you will do well to remember that in your trailing."

"Han, sahib," the Sikh muttered and a few moments later brought the car to a stop where woods came down to the road. Wentworth gave him the two grenades that remained, and for a moment the two men stood together beside the car. Then Wentworth thrust out his hand, gripped the hard palm of the Sikh.

"God guard you," he said formally.

The Sikh *salaamed*, lifted the ape to his shoulder and strode off into darkness.

WENTWORTH SPRANG behind the wheel and sent it roaring back across the city. Several times, he was forced to circle marauding bodies of Blancos and once he joined briefly in a battle where civilians were beleaguered in their home. But he could not delay long. He must reach Frankfort and the governor. It was vain to hope that a telephone communication from an unknown would carry weight, but if he could reach the man personally....

He frowned briefly at the thought that perhaps the Blancos would be before him at the airport, but he could see no purpose in such a raid, and it was at the other extreme of the city from their apparent point of ingress. Nevertheless, his eyes strained ahead as he streaked clear of the city limits and shot out along the straight highway that led to the airport. Already, he could spot the far-off sprinkling of red lights that marked the high danger spots about the field, and a plane was circling to a landing.

Wentworth trod on the gas. He did not know how many planes were stored at the airport. In any case, he did not want to delay even while a motor was warmed. It was possible he might make a deal with whoever was handling that ship. He stared at it, frowning. There was something damnably familiar about that plane!

As its bulk came against the landing-lights of the field, a cry burst from his lips. Surely, there were not two such amphibians in the country! That ship was his own! His heart leaped with the certainty that if the plane indeed was his, then it was Nita van Sloan who sat at the controls. But why should she be here?

Wentworth fretted at the slowness of his car, though the speedometer needle was wavering above eighty. He braked violently for the turn into the airport road, gassed while the car still rocked and shot past the parking-line out onto the field itself. The plane was motionless on the ground now and the pilot was climbing down... By the heavens, it was Nita! No other woman had that proud grace of carriage, that confidence in her tread. He hammered out a series of short and long blasts on the horn, and Nita swung toward the car, began to run.

Eagerness parted Wentworth's lips in a smile, but there was worry at the back of his mind. Apprehension over his safety might have brought Nita here, but he was afraid there was another more ominous reason. He slued the car to a halt, and an instant later had gathered Nita into his arms.

"Darling!" he cried. "In the name of Heaven, what brings you to this hell spot?"

Nita was clinging to him with a warmth that betrayed her

fears for him, but at his words he felt her stiffen in his embrace. She pushed away and her violet eyes were wide with fright, her cheeks pale.

"Hell spot?" she whispered. "Dick, do you mean… it has struck here, too?"

Wentworth's hands gripped her arms tightly. "Too? Then they've attacked New York!"

Nita's head jerked in a stiff nod. "Some beast-things that bullets don't seem able to stop," she rushed on. "They swarmed on a crowded subway platform tonight. Where they came from, no one knows—apparently, out of the earth. Before they were exterminated, they had killed more than two hundred people. It was an awful thing! I tried to get you by telephone at the Hill House and you had never arrived. Stanley Kirkpatrick wants you to get back to New York as soon as possible. I… I came as fast as I could."

"Good!" Wentworth approved. Things in New York must be serious indeed if Commissioner of Police Kirkpatrick urged his immediate return!

"I believe the governor can control things here," he said rapidly, "if he puts the whole area under martial law, but it may be difficult to persuade him. I'm glad you brought the plane…."

His words chopped off and he felt Nita shudder violently.

"What was that?" she asked, and even her voice trembled.

Wentworth peered frantically into the shadows, while he answered. "That," he whispered, "was the rallying cry of the Blancos! Quick, we must get to your plane!"

HE SCOOPED Nita into his arms and began to spring for

the ship. He knew, without question, that the arrival of the Blancos was no accident. Either he had been trailed, or they were after the ship. Abruptly, he skidded to a halt, a wild curse on his lips. Even as he ran, a single Blanco crept out from behind the ship.

Wentworth threw up his gun to fire—and didn't. Against one of the beast-men, he might use the automatic effectively, but another half-dozen of the creatures slouched into sight. The lights glittered on the slaughterous knives in their hands.

Wentworth whipped about, pelting back toward the car. Nita said no word, but ran swiftly beside him. A gun glinted in her hand, and something like pain twitched Wentworth's heart at the thought of how futile that weapon, and even Nita's splendid courage, would be in the face of these brute-things. So far, there were no Blancos about the car. Unless that, too, were blocked, they could escape....

Wentworth scarcely choked back the groan that rose to his lips. The Blancos were not about the car, but there was a solid corps of a score or more trotting along the highway toward the airport. He caught the glint of the chain leashes that bound them, heard the vicious thwack of a circling whip bite into their flesh. Those, then, were riflemen! God, what chance had he and Nita....

He flung himself behind the wheel of the car, kicked it into motion, but did not attempt the highway. Instead, he charged directly for the plane and the men around it. If he could put that between himself and the rifle squad, there might be a chance of pushing the car over fields to another road! The engine raced in second gear—the speedometer swung to forty, up toward fifty… The monsters about the plane were moving forward to the attack. A hoarse scream wailed across the field.

"Don't shoot," Wentworth threw at Nita, "except in extremity. Wounds only madden them and make them more ferocious."

His eyes were taking swift account of the Blancos ahead. Six men—and a wide field in which to maneuver. If he could not circle them… Another scream jerked his glance to the right. A second contingent was converging from that side! Furiously, Wentworth spun the wheel in the opposite direction—but the six he had been dodging were directly in his path. He drove the sedan directly at the leader.

With sudden inspiration, he slammed his palm on the horn. The Blanco stopped, mouth sagging open, and Wentworth hit him that way. The jar flung the car heavily to the left, but the Blanco was driven violently back, sent skidding a dozen feet along the earth. The blow had slowed the car and before Wentworth could gain headway, the other five Blancos closed in!

A knife swiped viciously at him, and he snapped a shot that rang on steel. He deflected the blade, but the Blanco's fist, gripping the hilt, caught him above the ear and drove him violently forward over the wheel. Beside him, Nita screamed wildly. He fought to lift his head and gun, got a bleared picture of a Blanco's arms about Nita, tearing her from the car! He brought up his gun, but his eyes were bleared. He dared not fire for a long moment. When, finally, he could, he hammered a bullet into the back of the Blanco's neck.

Before Wentworth could even see the result of that shot,

another of the white brutes came between him and Nita, leaped toward the car. Wentworth squeezed off a shot. He could hear Nita's scream, high and clear, above the hoarse rage of the Blancos.

"Save yourself, Dick!" she cried. "Save yourself! They won't harm me!"

Harm her! God, he had seen what they did to women! A knife slashed at Wentworth. The wounded Blanco had thrust himself half through the open window of the car on the opposite side. His bestial face—foam about the gnashing teeth, small pinkish eyes glaring—was within two feet of Wentworth. The knife… Wentworth fired desperately.

Out of the tail of his eye, he caught a glimpse of the plane dead ahead. He wrenched, one-handed, at the wheel while he fired again—and it was not enough. Straight into the fuselage of the plane, the car charged. The ship reared. Wentworth saw the heavy nose twist around, saw the propeller sheer toward him like a giant Blanco's knife, then pain struck through all his body.

Blazing light and darkness slammed into his skull. He knew that he was flying through space, but did not know when he struck the earth. He knew only that, in that last half-conscious moment, he heard once more Nita's despairing cry.

"Save yourself, Dick!"

The rest was silence—a ringing black void in which consciousness of everything… vanished.

CHAPTER 6
BATTLE OF BEASTS

THROUGH MILES of blackness, Wentworth's will drove him back to consciousness. Fire was inside his skull and the first twitch of abortive movement sent pain in hot waves over his body. But he persisted and, finally, his eyes opened on darkness. Cautiously, he moved his head. Spots of red light against the sky told him he was still at the airport, but the ground lights were out. A feeble chirping came to his ears and after an incredible time he identified it as the shrilling of frogs in a near-by marsh. There was no other sound.

"Nita!" Wentworth gasped.

He boosted himself up with trembling arms and nausea retched him. He persisted and presently was swaying on his feet. He lay almost fifty feet from the tangled wreckage of car and plane. The propeller had sheared through the roof and the decapitated body of the Blanco Wentworth had fought still draped grotesquely over the door. That was all. Wentworth sagged on the running-board of the car and buried his head in his hands.

When, finally he pried himself loose from the car, the eastern sky was almost imperceptibly lightening. His steps were erratic, but eventually they carried him toward the administration buildings and the hangars. Men's twisted, mutilated bodies were crumpled everywhere, like discarded rags. Once he stumbled across the body of a Blanco, torn by more than twenty bullets.

It seemed hours before Wentworth found a car and, from the bodies of the dead, found a key that would fit it. But at long last, he was behind the wheel and had the auto rolling. He knew where he was going in a dim way—toward those southern hills where first he had encountered the Blancos. Somewhere there he would pick up the trail that led to Nita and the fiends behind these atrocities. Somewhere....

There were great blanks in his memory of that drive. Once he remembered dimly that he circled a charred area of the city on whose outskirts a swarm of Blancos still ravaged houses and killed. He drove through a street choked with the bodies of men and women, where the few scattered corpses of the Blancos stood out whitely. His memory held the sound of screams, of distant, scattered shooting—and then no more. Then he found himself suddenly on a rutted hill road, standing beside a motionless car, with the hot sun of noon beating down upon him. He realized he was faint with exhaustion and hunger.

Whether he had followed some trail, or whether he was simply pushing more deeply into the hills he did not know. He tried to start the car, and the starter whirred and whirred without result. Out of gas. Wentworth began a slow climb along the road. It was white, gritty with limestone. Near the crest of the hill, he found a deserted cabin in whose yard a child lay, terribly dead. He stood staring down at it. Plainly, the Blancos had passed this way. He staggered on into the cabin, found food.

Afterward, he went on more rapidly. The thought of Nita stabbed him like a dull knife... Nita had said that in New York, the Blancos had seemed to come "out of the earth." The phrase was accidental, but Wentworth glimpsed in it a hint of the truth. Kentucky's limestone hills were honeycombed with caverns, would provide an ideal hiding place for the swarms of the Blancos.

Dusk found him miles farther into the hills, and he began a desperate plan he had fixed upon.

HE STRIPPED off his clothing and sprinkled hair and body with the white limestone dust of the road. He shredded his shirt and bound it about his waist, concealed in it his automatic and the few rounds of spare ammunition which remained. Then he threw back his head and uttered a scream, hoarse and wild and penetrating—the rallying scream of the Blancos! If he could not find the Blancos, they could at least find him.

The very hills seemed to shudder with the sound, and the echoes sent it crashing back against his ear-drums. There was silence for a long while, then somewhere in the distance, a whip-poor-will took up its lonely whistled plaint. That was all.

Wentworth plodded on, shoes loosely on his feet, ready to be discarded at an instant's notice. At intervals, he threw back his head and uttered the cry. The night turned chill, and the moon thrust its silvery rim above the hills, and still Wentworth shoved on.

He had left roads behind and there were no more than game-trails through thick woods that thicketed the rocky hills. He reached the top of a sharp rise, clambered up a low cliff that thrust starkly out of the trees. On its utmost reach, he paused again to voice his cry. There was desperation in his tones, a pleading of which perhaps he was not even aware. His throat was hoarse with his screaming, and the sound of it, tearing the night apart, startled him with its wildness. Afterward, he stood staring out over the wildness into which he had plunged so hopelessly, a mournful, naked figure of a man....

HE HAD turned to resume his desperate march when the sound reached him, so faint that he paused, half-thinking it an echo, half-believing it some trick of his imagination. Then it came again, thinned by distance—the rallying scream of the Blancos! Once more, Wentworth tipped back his head and set the echoes crazy with his cry... and once more the answer came.

Hope thrilled through Wentworth. He sprinted back from the rock into the fastnesses of the forest, slipped and rolled fifty feet down a steep slope before he recovered his footing. After that, he moved more slowly, changing his frantic dash into a jog-trot as he bored even farther south toward the sound of that cry. Impossible to tell what lay ahead—perhaps instant, bloody death or long, primitive torture. But it was hope, the contact with the enemy for which he had struggled—and the knowledge lent him new strength. If he could, he would mingle with the Blancos, seek out their lair and the men who led them, find Nita....

The time came when he topped a rise, hidden in trees, and knew that the screaming of the Blancos was no more than two hundreds yards away—on the crest of the next ridge.

He struggled to accomplish the thing that made him a master of disguise, to bury himself in the identity he had assumed. He was a Blanco, straggling back alone from the raid—a beast-man intent only on rejoining his kind and lonely in the darkness of the in-pressing night. He cried out again and again and crashed recklessly through the undergrowth. With a final scream, he burst out into a narrow clearing where a half-dozen of the Blancos crouched on their haunches, or stood in slouching postures that were divided between menace and fear.

Wentworth stopped just inside the clearing. He stiffened his body, lips snarled back from teeth. It seemed to him that he had reverted centuries in the few minutes he had rushed up the hill. This might be a scene out of ages past—cavemen crouched about the entrance of then den and a newcomer, one of their own kind, but a stranger, crashing out of the encircling forest. Wentworth's hands were empty; those of the others clutched knives and clubs. Wentworth stood motionless, glowering, waiting—for death, or welcome.

One of the men, the largest, rose to his feet and came forward a pace, a heavy club half-lifted in his fist.

"I am Jed!" he growled. "I am the strongest man in the world!"

The words were barely recognizable to Wentworth, coming forth, thick-throated and malformed, like imitative sounds uttered by a beast. Jed's face was twisted by a half-healed knife scar that just missed his left eye. He beat his chest with a half-clenched fist and his jaw began to champ in anger.

"I am Jed!" he cried. "No man can kill me!"

Wentworth swore under his breath. This was primitive tribalism in its lowest form. This man had subdued the others by brute strength. He was their leader, and Wentworth realized that if he wished to remain with this group, he must conquer him! Conquer a beast-man whom a heart-shot would not stop!

It might be wiser to retreat... but it had already gone beyond that. Even if Wentworth so desired, he could not now escape these Blancos. His own lips writhed in an echo of the man's rage.

"I am Dick!" Wentworth snarled back at him. "I am stronger than Jed!"

His eyes flicked for a moment to the others. Would they join in an attack upon him, or would this be a battle between himself and Jed? He perceived no immediate menace in the others, and a glimmering of hope came to him. If he could kill Jed quickly, he could make himself leader of these men! Then his eyes swung back to the snarling beast-man. Kill him? But he must!

"Dick is stronger than Jed!" he roared at the beast-man.

He struck his chest, tipped back his head and screamed. While the sound still tore his throat, Jed charged, the club upraised and ready for a smashing blow.

Wentworth sprang abruptly forward. He balled, dived, hit Jed's ankles with shoulder and hip, and heaved up. With a wild cry, Jed crashed to the ground. Instantly, Wentworth was on his feet. He jumped high and drove down, stiff-legged with his heels into the small of Jed's back! Something gave under that driving impact. Jed screamed, rolled, and lashed out with the club. It caught Wentworth a glancing blow on the thigh. Flesh split under the impact, and Wentworth was hurled a half dozen feet. He would have fallen except that his shoulders brought up hard against a tree. And Jed was on his feet, charging again!

Wentworth's hand was achingly tight upon the butt of the gun in his loin cloth. Did he dare to use it—or would it betray him to the other Blancos and bring a concerted attack?

Jed was making the club whistle in a wild arc about his head as he leaped once more to the attack. He dodged past Jed, jammed the muzzle of the automatic hard against the man's side and squeezed the trigger. Jed's roar of pain drowned out the flesh-muffled discharge of the automatic. His whirl was lightning-swift and Wentworth barely dodged a second deadly swing of the club! A .45 caliber bullet, ripping through his vitals at point-blank range, had not even slowed the Blanco! With great bounds, he pursued Wentworth across the narrow clearing.

Wentworth dodged aside and, when Jed blundered past, dragged a foot to trip him. That was a mistake! Jed's heavy foot closed on the back of Wentworth's heel with a grip like a hand! With a roar of triumph, he whipped up the mighty club! Wentworth went flat down on his back.

With the quickness of thought, he braced his other foot against the knee of the leg that held him prisoner, and thrust with all the strength of his powerful back and thigh muscles. The leverage drove Jed back a full stride. His blow missed, and Wentworth, free, rolled to his feet. As he rose, he caught up a jagged fragment of rock—and, when Jed charged again, hurled it squarely into the beast-man's face!

That blow, which would have smashed the skull of an ordinary man, barely slowed the Blanco. But when he came on, he was half-blinded. Wentworth at last had the chance he sought. As the club swung down, he seized the Blanco's wrist and hurled himself backward to the earth while he drove both feet hard into the creature's groin! For only an instant, Wentworth clung to the wrist, then he released it and sent Jed pin-wheeling, screaming hoarsely, a dozen feet through the air. Jed fell heavily on a cluster of jagged rocks, but his roar was as much rage as pain! He staggered to his feet, almost before Wentworth himself could rise. There were jagged, bloodless tears in his shoulders and chest. The rock Wentworth had hurled had crushed out an eye, and his club-arm dangled, broken, from the shoulder. But he *charged* again!

Wentworth gripped the automatic in his belt and waited his chance. As the beast-man blundered toward him, he dodged—and slipped! With a scream of triumph, the Blanco threw his heavy body upon Wentworth's back and a powerful arm clamped under his chin, wrenched his head upward. Instantly, paralyzing pain sliced through Wentworth's spine. The Blanco's knees were digging into the small of his back and that single arm, beneath his chin, would snap his spine like a dead branch! And Wentworth's gun was pinned under him, held down by the double weight of his own body and the murder-mad beast upon his back!

CHAPTER 7
CAGES OF THE DAMNED!

IN WENTWORTH'S ears were the hoarse, triumphant screams of Jed and before his eyes flickered the leaping, dancing bodies of the other Blancos, glorying in his victory. His breath was cut off by that crushing forearm under his throat and his back was an agony beyond bearing. Still, Wentworth's coldly calculating brain clicked on.

With what seemed to Wentworth the slowness of a night-mare, he got his left hand up and groped until he found the knotted fist of Jed. With dimming consciousness, he forced up one finger of Jed's fist and put all his fading strength into a frantic effort to shred that finger from Jed's hand! He heard a whimper of pain, and blunt teeth fastened on his ear. Under his twisting, levering fingers, he felt bones break and, deliberately, he ground the broken bones into flesh.

With a scream, Jed jerked savagely to loosen the hold. Wentworth twisted his head free of that punishing grip and got his gun hand loose. His head was slammed violently against the earth. A hand gouged at his face and the gaping teeth of the Blanco lunged for his throat! Wentworth jammed the muzzle of the gun into that open mouth and began pulling the trigger!

Wentworth felt that his eyes would pop from their sockets under the gouging fingers of the beast-man. He was dimly conscious of the jerk of recoil in his gun hand, of the screams of the beast-men about him. At what point he became aware that the heavy body that ground him down was relaxing, he did not know, but he recognized that he had won—and that he must get instantly to his feet. Within moments after Jed had ceased to live, he must get to his feet—or some other Blanco would seize a chance to become leader!

How he managed it, Wentworth never knew, but he pushed aside the relaxing body of the Blanco, thrust the gun into the rag about his waist and reeled upright. On braced feet, he confronted the others. He slammed a fist against his chest.

"I am Dick!" he said thickly. "I am Dick!" He shouted, "Dick is the strongest man in the world!"

He tipped back his head and screamed his challenge at the moon-whitened skies! The other Blancos cringed from him and Wentworth knew that he had won. He ate meat that would have turned his stomach at any other time.

"Dick sleep," he rumbled, then, "Dick sleep with one eye! You come in, Dick kill!"

The lesson was enough. The Blancos chattered out hoarse words of assent and Wentworth flung himself down to sleep.

IN THREE hours' time, he was awake again and prodding the other Blancos into movement. First, he led the Blancos, then gradually allowed one of the others to take the lead. It was his intention that they should take him to some larger concentration of Blancos where he could find the way to the criminals who ruled them, and then to Nita.

The Blanco in the lead roamed without direction for a considerable while, but, striking a wider trail, swung into a jog trot and the others followed. That went on endlessly and birds were twittering with the first restlessness of dawn, when finally—far ahead—Wentworth heard the scream of a Blanco.

Instantly, the full chorus of his own party answered it, and then speed quickened. Wentworth kept pace with them. If he kept among a huddle of others, he hoped to escape detection. When they ran out into the Blanco-crowded clearing against a jutting cliff, he drew them around him with a rumbled order.

"Get food," he ordered one.

His eyes quested rapidly over the scene. The Blancos were

DR. RAND

DR. LIEBERLING

drawn together in small groups and clusters like his own, eating. A narrow cave mouth showed in the face of the cliff and, on each side of it, a Blanco stood with a ready whip in his hand. Whenever one of the wandering beast-men approached too closely, the whip lashed out. There were squeals of pain, but no resistance. But though Wentworth sought at length, his eyes found no trace of any living being other than Blancos in the clearing. It was like a cave-man scene.

The man he had sent out returned with a half of a roasted pig and Wentworth tore loose a section for himself, grunted at the

JANET RAND

JACK DAWSON

others. Instantly, they fell to upon the meat and Wentworth was once more free to study out his position.

Once more, Wentworth fell to pondering upon the strange vitality of the men. A sudden memory flashed across his brain. Janet Rand had admitted that her father artificially created albinos! Was it possible that these brutes were the men who had vanished in the Kentucky hills, converted by some cruel alchemy to their present form? Suppose the process, as devised by Rand, had the result of debasing, brutalizing those to whom it was applied? Suppose it caused a thickening of the blood which, quickly coagulating, closed the wounds?

As the full enormity of his deductions struck him, Wentworth felt an overpowering rage sweep through his veins. Men, white men, kidnaped and converted to beasts so that they, in then turn, could slaughter other civilized men—for the greed of a few who held them in power! It was a fiendish conception, but, instinctively, Wentworth knew it was true. His mind quested back

over the men who might be responsible for this horror—Dr. Rand or the vanishing Hans Lieberling. Wentworth frowned a moment with the recollection that Major Hascomb, of the national guard, on leaving the city, had apparently failed to notify his subordinate. That might be merely carelessness—or it might be something more furtive and ugly!

Wentworth was jerked out of his thoughts by a loud cracking of whips. A dozen more of the whip-armed Blancos had issued from the cave mouth and they made a slow, circling movement of the clearing, swinging their lashes brutally. The other Blancos started to their feet, whimpering, and slowly converged on the cave mouth. Wentworth moved with them. It came to him painfully that the touch of a metal-tipped whip on his back could betray his masquerade in an instant. He would bleed!

A bedlam of angry screaming rose from the Blancos but they began to duck into the cave mouth. Wentworth wedged himself into their midst. Presently, a few flaring torches illuminated the high vault of a central cavern, luridly. Groups of Blancos began to settle down on their haunches against the walls, hundreds of them.

How many such caverns hidden in the fastnesses of the Kentucky hills held such swarms of Blancos? How could he know whether he had succeeded in finding a central cavern? This might be merely an outpost.

WENTWORTH WANDERED off into the darkness of the back cavern, spying out small tunnel mouths that might lead anywhere—or nowhere. Then, a thrill of hope sprang up. One larger tunnel mouth was guarded by two Blancos with whips! Cautiously, Wentworth crept nearer. He could not risk discovery, but he must know. Was this merely the lair of the Blancos' leader—or was it the headquarters of the entire organization of criminals?

Wentworth crept closer, narrowing his eyes to peer beyond that whip-guarded mouth. There was torch light beyond, and he made out a steel-slatted gate set across the entrance! Even as he stared, he heard the beat of booted feet, running swiftly, heard a woman's faint cry of despair. God, were his ears playing him tricks? It couldn't be Nita. It couldn't be....

His heart leaped into his throat. Now he could see, through those slatted bars, the woman's form speeding up that narrow tunnel-way, could hear the shouts of pursuers! Wentworth's lips opened in a cry of encouragement, and he lunged toward the guards with their whips. He saw Nita reach the bars and shake them, futilely, then her white face seemed to be peering directly into his.

"Nita!" he called. "Fight them off! I'm coming!"

"Run!" Nita cried. "They won't harm me. They want me to run a plane. Tomorrow night, they attack Franklin! Run, Dick...."

The two guards were advancing toward him with lashing whips. Wentworth whipped out his gun—and pain slashed across his shoulders! A whiplash had bitten into his back! He whirled and there were five whip-armed men behind him. Before he could even level his gun, a whiplash wrapped around his gun wrist and paralyzed it. Another twined about his throat and cut off his breath. He fought frantically, but with fading strength. He managed to squeeze off a shot and then a blow on the head smashed him to his knees.

"That's no Blanco!" a man's startled, thick voice cried. "Look, he bleeds!"

That was the last word Wentworth heard before another blow smashed him into unconsciousness.

CHAPTER 8
WHEN MEN'S SOULS DIE!

FOR A long while after he recovered consciousness, Wentworth did not stir at all. He was aware of men's muttering voices about him and of the clanking of many chains. He realized that there were chains on his own ankles and wrists, and that he was fastened to a larger one half-buried in sand. More than that was hidden from him, for he was in absolute darkness. Now and then he caught a mumbled phrase.

A man said hoarsely, "Tomorrow we get that damned needle again."

Another answered, "It hurts like hell. What's the idea? They sure to God aren't afraid we'll get sick."

Wentworth's lips tightened at the words. He could guess better than they the purpose of the hypodermics! If his theory was right, those needles were converting them into albino beasts! That such would be his own fate, he did not question.

Wentworth forced his aching body erect and a man near him muttered, "The Blanco is coming to!"

He drove words past his thickened tongue. "How long have I been unconscious?"

"How long, hell!" the man next to him laughed raucously. "You ain't going no place."

Silently, Wentworth felt over his manacles. They were smooth metal, not large and so probably of tool steel. The chain was rougher and the links thick. He ground one on the sandy floor, where he lay, for several moments, and, afterward, it seemed to him it was appreciably smoother. The chains, then, were soft iron! A grim smile twitched his lips. By a week of constant scrubbing, he might wear it thin enough to break—but the needle would be thrust into his body tomorrow!

"You can't do nothing with them chains," the man beside him spoke. "It'd take a month."

Wentworth stared toward the voice. "Can you see me?" he asked abruptly.

"See you?" the man rumbled. "Of course. After you been in here awhile you can see all right."

Wentworth shook his head, still staring toward the man.

"What you shaking your head about?" the man asked irritably.

"Nothing," Wentworth said quietly, but he knew now that the man spoke the truth—and he realized another more formidable fact. The man's transition into an albino had already advanced to the point that his eyes were affected! It was that which enabled him to see in the dark!

"You were talking about a needle," Wentworth began again. "How many injections have they given you?"

"One," the man replied, and his voice was thick, bestial. No doubt about him!

Once—and his eyes were the eyes of an albino and he spoke with the voice of a Blanco! Tomorrow, Wentworth would receive that injection—unless he could escape! Despair welled up in his heart. Somewhere in this vast catacomb, Nita was a prisoner, too, but she would be more carefully guarded than ever after her break for freedom. He could hope for nothing from her. Rather, she must look to him for rescue!

What was it Nita had cried when he had made that abortive attempt to save her? Franklin was to be looted, ravaged by the Blanco hordes. She was used as a pilot. Even while he lay here, helpless, doomed to undergo this slaughter of the soul that was worse than outright death, Franklin's thousands might be dying under the onslaught of Blancos! Frenzy gripped his brain, but he fought against it. He grasped the chain that bound him and began steadily to rub it in the sand. Hopeless as it was, he must try that slim chance.

For hours he could not estimate, Wentworth scrubbed at the

iron link, taking regular periods of rest. The men about him slept and awoke again. His knuckles were raw from the abrasion of the sand and his arms grew numb with fatigue, but still Wentworth labored on.

WHEN THE first faint tracery of torch glow began to shine into the chamber where he was imprisoned, Wentworth was forced to desist. He strained his eyes to inspect his work. The link was about three-eights of an inch thick and he had worn away perhaps a sixth of that thickness. If he could continue his efforts interrupted for five more such sessions, he might be able to snap the link. But those torches meant that already the men were coming to inject him, and these others, with the solution that would convert him into a beast!

By the increasing light of the torches, Wentworth peered about him. The vault of the cavern's ceiling was beyond the reach of the flaring torches. The walls threw back a thousand scin-tillant gleams and weird shadows twisted and writhed among stalactites and stalagmites gnarled into fantastic forms. After that single injection, the men were bleached and sullen. Already, bestial lines twisted their faces out of human semblance. The second injection undoubtedly would complete their transfor-mation into Blancos. Could he rouse them to revolt?

"You know what that needle does?" he demanded of the man next to him. "It changes you into a Blanco! Look at your hands—look at the men about you!"

The man blinked at him stupidly, shielding his eyes against the encroaching light.

The lash struck at Wentworth again and again.

THE GREY HORDE CREEPS

"A Blanco, huh?" he grunted thickly. "Well, if I was a Blanco I wouldn't be chained here. They get to go out."

"Fool!" Wentworth snapped at him. "Don't you realize that your own family will run from you if they see you again? Don't you know your wife…."

The man threw back his head in a roar of laughter. "That's swell, just swell! Hey, guys!" He turned to the others around him. "This mug says the injections make us into Blancos so our own wives won't know us! And he expects us to kick at that!"

Shouts of laughter went up from the men. A few trembled and peered with fright at the approach of the torches, wholly visible now—but that was all. Wentworth turned to watch the men with the torches. There were a dozen of them, all Blancos! Wentworth frowned and stared intently. It didn't seem possible that any persons converted into a Blanco would have enough intelligence to wield a hypodermic needle. Even those who had carried rifles had been on chains and driven by whips.

Sharply, Wentworth's head jerked about. Somewhere in the darkness behind him, he had caught a low-pitched call.

"*Sahib!*" it came softly. "*Sahib!*"

"Ram Singh!" Wentworth gasped. Swiftly, he spoke a few words in Punjabi, telling Ram Singh about the injections and their purpose—that Nita, too, was a prisoner.

"Did the ape lead you here?" he asked.

"*Han, sahib!*" said Ram Singh. "A Blanco—one of the body-guard—carries the ape always on his shoulder. And the message is gone from his collar!"

So Dr. Rand was here! Wentworth had a clue, but he was totally unable even to get his information to the outside world.

"Be of good courage," he called to Ram Singh, still speaking in Punjabi, and, abruptly, one of the torch-bearers sprang from line and came leaping through the ranks of the chained prisoners. The lash reached out and slashed across Wentworth's chest.

"Dog!" the man rasped. "Who were you talking to in—in that outlandish language?"

Wentworth stared up at the Blanco. His lips had not moved when he had spoken those words—and suddenly Wentworth understood. These were not Blancos, but men in the garb of Blancos and those distorted bestial faces were… *masks!*

"I spoke to myself, *sahib,*" Wentworth muttered. "It is a habit of mine!"

The lash struck at him again, and Wentworth bit his lips to choke back a cry of pain. The man in Blanco disguise laughed harshly.

"There is a cure for that!" he rasped, and turning he shouted at the others in the procession. "Here is the man to inject first!"

Then they came rushing at him, overpowering him—it was all over.

WENTWORTH SURGED to his feet, but the chains held him so that he was only half-erect—ankles and wrists bound shortly together. The whistling lash cut down across his shoulders and drove him to his knees. He heard Ram Singh shout in inarticulate rage and then the lash beat across his skull. Hands gripped his shoulders and there was sharp pain at the base of his skull. Good God, the needle!

89

"The idiot had broken the needle!" A man cried, then the lashes tore at Wentworth's back. He did not know when they ceased, but presently he was conscious of his surroundings.

He had accomplished nothing except to weaken himself for the labor which lay ahead. He had a double reason for speed now. Not only must he escape to warn the people, to lead an overwhelming force to this hell-hole of the hills, but he must do these things before... before the damnable fluid they had pumped into his veins got in its deadly work. Once that struck, he would become like these others about him. Even his mighty will might not be able to resist the general bestialization of his body and soul.

Presently, he recognized that the cave was brighter, that the light was whiter. He pushed half-erect and saw another procession hurrying out of a black tunnel mouth across the chamber. A shout rose against his teeth. For in that smaller, hurrying group, he recognized two things. One of the Blancos carried a white ape on his shoulder... and Nita walked among them!

There were five Blancos with Nita, and she walked beside one of them, an erect, long-striding man. The other four were grouped protectingly about them. Wentworth's eyes narrowed as he watched. Beyond any doubt, this was a high leader of the Blancos.

Nita called and ran forward. These other trials Wentworth had borne, but the sight of Nita was almost too much for him; the thought that the day would come when she would shrink from him as from a wild beast—if he lived that long! Determination rose grimly in his soul. He would smash these hell-fiends, but when the beast signs crept out in this body that had served him so well—that very day, he would destroy it!

Nita dropped on her knees beside Wentworth, cried out at the wounds which scarred his body.

"Oh, Dick," she whispered. "Dick, lover...."

Wentworth looked beyond her to the Blanco leader and his guard and, though the man's face was hidden behind a bestial mask, Wentworth knew that he smiled.

"The woman has asked for your life," the voice came out, thick and muffled, sneering. "She is valuable to us—an expert pilot—so we have come to an agreement. She is to fly for us, and you will be our hostage."

Wentworth said steadily, "Ram Singh is a prisoner here. I do not think they have injected him yet." He waited, silent.

"Ram Singh!" Nita cried. She turned toward the Blanco leader.

"What, another man to be rescued?" he jeered, then shrugged. "We have many Blancos." He lifted his voice, and two whip-bearing men trotted toward him.

"Free this man," the leader directed. "There is also a Sikh here, whom you will free and bring to me."

The whip-men stared at Wentworth and from behind the mask came laughter. "That one—" he indicated Wentworth—"already has received an injection."

Nita cried out and her arms tightened convulsively about Wentworth.

Already Wentworth felt unclean, that he should shrink from Nita's clasp. Freed from the gang-chain, he still could not stand erectly because of the short length that bound ankles to wrists. The wounds of his back were exquisite torture. He carried his head high, nevertheless, as he shuffled off with the procession and presently, Ram Singh, too, was beside him. The leader's taunting voice reached his ears....

"Our scientists are working on an antidote," he said. "It is barely possible they may perfect it in time to help your lover, Nita. Whether he receives it will depend entirely on how well you serve us!"

Nita's head was high. "I will do what I promised, no more," she said quietly. "I will pilot your plane, but I will not take part in any attacks upon the helpless people you slaughter!"

"Quite right, Nita," Wentworth said quietly.

The leader laughed loudly. "Heroic to the end!" he sneered. "You will feel differently about it when you are a Blanco!"

Wentworth felt the tremor of Nita's hand on his arm, but neither of them answered. The winding tunnel through which they moved, enlarged in places, had once been the course of an underground stream. Twice, they had passed steel gates set in the living rock, each guarded by whip-men.

WENTWORTH WINCED as a sudden weight struck his shoulder, then smiled as a small ape face peered around into his and a small, furry arm clutched at his neck. It was the white ape of Dr. Rand, which had sprung from the Blanco's shoulder to his own. Wentworth made small clucking noises at the animal and, when the Blanco reached for it, the ape resisted being taken, raising a high chattering that echoed weirdly in the narrow tunnel. Wentworth studied the Blanco with the ape, but the man wore no mask. He was a real Blanco.

After a dragging eternity, the procession halted and Wentworth found himself confronting a small side-cavern converted into a cell by steel bars and a door set across its front. Wentworth was thrust in; the door clanged shut. Nita smiled bravely at him through the bars.

"Don't give up hope, Dick," she said. "Men like these can't survive for long. I... I'll win that antidote for you!"

Wentworth smiled, touched her hand. He did not believe in the antidote's existence. It was merely trickery by which the leader planned to keep her loyal to him, but Wentworth did not have the heart to rob Nita of that fragment of hope.

He said, quietly, "Of course, dear. I'll see you soon at Franklin...."

"Franklin," Nita said, a sob in her throat, "was... destroyed last night. It was... awful!"

"Come!" the leader said impatiently.

Nita pressed her lips to Wentworth's between the bars, and turned away. The light died into blackness, but still Wentworth could hear the faint clanking of Ram Singh's chains and the shrill chattering of the ape.

Wentworth sagged upon the sand floor and his proud head for once bowed in something very like despair. Nita's heroic effort had come too late to save him from the injection and he was immured more hopelessly than ever. Even if he freed himself of the chains, those steel bars held him in. And beyond this were guarded gates and a cavern crowded with Blancos. Franklin was destroyed, two cities wiped off the map so that a few men might grow rich on thievery and slaughter, New York threatened. God alone knew what had happened there now. A full day had elapsed since Nita had sped here to bring the cry for help of Commissioner of Police Stanley Kirkpatrick. And Nita....

A sob rose in Wentworth's throat. What was the end of this for her, of New York, for the people of the nation....

CHAPTER 9
THE HOUR OF DOOM

IN NEW YORK, a man sat grim-faced behind his desk— as stern as if he defended a hopelessly beleaguered fortress. He clipped out crackling orders in an even, unemotional voice and the police he commanded flew to obey his commands. Those white ape-men had struck again in the subways, the third successive night, and the machine-gun reserves had rushed into battle—a fight in which they would die as surely as if they committed suicide.

The man swept up a telephone. "Wentworth's home," he ordered and waited while the connection went through. "Stanley Kirkpatrick speaking," he said crisply. "Have you any word yet?"

Something of the crispness went out of his poise as the answer came back. It was as if he knew that Wentworth would return if it were possible—that the failure meant that even Wentworth was beaten. If he could have known that Wentworth crouched in utter despair, in a nameless cavern, prisoner of the men he battled!

Kirkpatrick hung up slowly, staring blankly before him. He had thrown every man into battle who could help. Wentworth might know some means of overpowering these beast-men. No doubt that he had gone west to investigate them. Kirkpatrick pushed to his feet, a saturnine, deliberate man in precisely tailored clothing. Even in this moment of desperation, he paused beside his desk, for an instant, to pluck the gardenia he habitually wore from its holder on the desk and fasten it to his lapel. He knuckled his military mustache as he strode toward the door, then, and the grey above his temples found an echo in the drag of his usually brisk, military stride.

For years, he had been police commissioner of the city, held over from one administration to another because the people knew and relied on his honesty and would not have it otherwise. But he who had fought so many criminal alliances successfully felt a gnawing of despair now.

He threw back his shoulders, opened the door and went out. His special limousine, with its two-way radio communication system, was at the door, uniformed driver beside it, and Kirkpatrick sprang in.

"Herald Square," he ordered, and his voice rasped. "Make it fast!"

The siren rose to a shriek, and traffic skittered from the path of the red-eyed police car. Kirkpatrick sat with burning gaze, staring unseeingly at the streets through which he whirled. Unless he checked these beast-men, who sprang from God alone knew where, working their fearful havoc, these same streets would be desolate with terror. Long before he could reach the scene of the disaster, the thickly-crowded shopping district of Herald Square, the traffic slowed his car to a walk. Ambulances wailed and gonged their way through, painfully. Traffic police fought to clear the streets. Finally, Kirkpatrick sprang out and strode toward the subway kiosk—and stopped in his tracks. Even here, death had reached.

Sprawled brokenly across the steps was the body of a policeman and, half-covering him, the corpse of one of the white beast-men. One of the beast's legs had been virtually severed by machine-gun bullets, his back was stitched with the bloody marks where lead had torn completely through him—but he had fought on to smash the life from the policeman!

Kirkpatrick's eyes were bitter as blue ice as he strode on down the steps. He loved these men of his as if they were his own family; he had no other. In his heart was a shrinking at the sight

NITA VAN SLOAN •

he knew he must find below, but he pushed on. A sergeant was bounding up the steps. He stopped and saluted.

"We've killed the last one, sir," he gasped. "Killed them, but... Oh, God!" His knees buckled and, still conscious, he slid to the steps.

Kirkpatrick's eyes swept the man. One arm dangled crookedly from the shoulder socket. His uniform was ripped and blood streamed from a gash in his throat.

"Thank you, Sergeant," Kirkpatrick said steadily.

Two civilians dashed past and Kirkpatrick's hand shot out

to stop them. "Take this officer to an ambulance, at once!" he snapped at them.

Terror haunted the faces of the two men. They stared back over their shoulders at the dimness of the subway, and whimperingly obeyed. The sergeant struggled to his feet, and Kirkpatrick strode on. Screams beat upon his ears—the screams of dying men and women. Hospital men hurried past him with covered stretchers on which red stains spread ominously. Three wounded policemen were helping among the others, injured more terribly than themselves. Ghastly, twisted things that had been human beings were huddled about the platform, and beside one of those pitiful things a child stood and cried and cried.

Kirkpatrick lifted the child into his arms, his grim face twisted. One of the policemen stood before him. Kirkpatrick's eyes went beyond him, swept the stalled train at the platform, saw the torn bodies of uniformed men and the huger mounds of the slain ape-men.

"All the rest," Kirkpatrick said slowly, "All but you three and Sergeant Kilroy...."

"Dead, sir," the policeman said thickly. "But we killed the beasts!"

FIFTEEN POLICEMEN slain! Kirkpatrick's eyes skimmed the platform, wincing. Fifteen police and fully fifty civilians dead! And the ape-men... no more than a dozen killed. Fresh men in blue were streaming down into the subway now, and Kirkpatrick gave crisp orders.

"Survivors who are able will report to headquarters after medical treatment," he said briefly. "I'll want to know all details of the fight. We must find some way…" He cut it off short and, still carrying the softly crying child, made his way up the steps. An angry man ran toward him as he reached the top.

"Why don't you protect us!" he screamed. "Why don't the police protect us! My wife…" His voice broke and sobs wrenched at his shoulders. A newspaperman's flashlight flung savage blue-white light over the scene. Kirkpatrick pushed through to his car, wordlessly. What answer could he make to that bereaved man, to a dozen more like him—that fifteen police had died? It was only their duty.

At headquarters, a swarm of newspapermen beset him. Kirkpatrick gave the child into a matron's care and faced the men.

"This attack is finished," he said slowly. "All of the beast-men were killed. Fifteen police died to do that. The number of civilians is unknown, but at least thirty of them are dead. Almost all of these were killed before police could get there—in the first two minutes. I am taking steps to guard against a recurrence of the disaster."

"What steps, Commissioner?" a newsman demanded.

Kirkpatrick frowned heavily. It was a question he had been asking himself. It seemed futile to patrol the subways with armed men. There was no guarantee that the next outbreak would be there, but the effort must be made. He told the newsmen that.

"I'll give out further details later," he added, and pushed wearily through their ranks to his office. The phone buzzed and he strode to it with sudden hope. If Wentworth were located….

"Hello? Stanley Kirkpatrick speaking… Hello, Governor." He fought to keep the despair out of his voice. "The national guard?

Well, it might help to allay panic. I'm going to put machine-gun patrols in all the subways. The people might feel safer if their defenders were in military uniform, though it's my belief, the police can do a better job. I'll get the mayor to ask you for the guardsmen."

He sat heavily at his desk, staring straight before him. Yes, he would put patrols in the subways—but they wouldn't help. Those beast-men could wipe out the thin line of sentries in a moment's time. It would be a patrol of death. God, if only he could learn something about the beast-men—how to fight them.

If he could get hold of Wentworth....

And far off in his hill prison, Wentworth sat hunched beneath the weight of his chains, behind steel bars. Dully, he repeated the fighting phrase which had pried him loose from so many hopeless prisons. He whispered aloud to himself, "I am not yet dead!"

There was no echoing lift of his heart. One thing at a time, he told himself. First get rid of the chains. Fumblingly, his fingers groped for the smooth place he had worn in a link of the chain. Without hope, he drove himself relentlessly on. The iron made a faint whispering against the sand. The echo seemed to make words in Wentworth's ears, words of despair, "Doomed... doomed... doomed...."

CHAPTER 10
"I AM NOT YET DEAD!"

WENTWORTH COULD not have told how long he labored before he became aware of a tapping, that echoed faintly along the tunnel, and identified the sounds as Morse code. Swiftly, he moved to the bars and clanked the chains against them in answer. After that, the message came swiftly—

AM IN CELL LIKE YOURS HUNDRED YARDS FARTHER ON. DAWSON, JANET RAND ALSO HERE. (SIGNED) RAM SINGH.

Wentworth frowned over that knowledge, as he tapped back a message of courage. If Dr. Rand were guilty, and wished to hide that fact even from his daughter, he might still imprison her for safety. He could make little of their imprisonment, except the certitude that the message he had sent by the ape had caused their capture. But he was losing precious time. He must work on the chains....

"Try to get free of chains!" he tapped back. *"Goodbye."*

Wentworth returned to his grinding at that one link, but somehow the task did not seem so hopeless now. If he could get out, free Dawson and Ram Singh... If he could get out! But while he labored so futilely here, the leader was planning God alone knew what further infamies! Days must pass before he could snap the chain and two nights had sufficed to destroy two cities and thousands of lives!

When Wentworth was forced to sleep, he awoke to feel tiny leathery hands plucking at his face and sat up in abrupt fright. Immediately, a shrill, terrified chattering broke out. Wentworth laughed softly. The white ape had come again! He made small clucking sounds in his throat, and the chattering stilled.

The ape returned to nestle on his shoulders, arms about Wentworth's neck. It clung there even when Wentworth renewed his work upon the chain… Abruptly, Wentworth stopped. He was conscious of another presence in the darkness, of eyes upon him!

"Who is there?" he said harshly.

A Blanco's rumbled tones answered, "I am Con. You have stolen Con's ape."

Wentworth strained his eyes but could see nothing at all. At least, the fluid injected into him had not yet started to work!

"If Con wants the ape," he said quietly, "Con can come in and get him."

He held his breath for the answer. Was the Blanco intelligent enough to know that he should not unlock the door of the cage? There was silence through long seconds while, apparently, the Blanco's slow mind assimilated the thought. Wentworth strained forward, waiting.

"Con no got key," the man said finally.

"Con can get key," Wentworth suggested softly. "Not let big boss know."

Silence dragged out again. Finally, the Blanco made a low throat noise, and the ape sprang from Wentworth's shoulder. Wentworth heard him scamper across the floor and through the bars, and footsteps moved away. Slowly, Wentworth's lips curved in a smile. The ape would return, now that it had found the way and another time, he would secure the animal. Also, he had planted an idea in the Blanco's mind that might, eventually, bear fruit. Wentworth returned to his task with renewed vigor.

ONCE DURING the day Wentworth was fed, and several

times messages came tapping along the corridor from Ram Singh. He was making slow progress on his chains. Dawson and the girl were not shackled. It was not long after this that Wentworth caught the distant gleam of moving torches and knew a procession was approaching. The lights meant more than that, for the Blancos needed no illumination. It meant that those who were coming along the corridor were the false, masked Blancos—perhaps the leader himself!

Wentworth hid the chain link on which he was working, beneath his wrist, and flung himself down on the sand. The beat of footsteps filled the corridor and above it came the clattering sound of the ape's gabble. A moment later, the group had stopped before his cell and Nita was clinging to the bars.

"Dick," she said rapidly, "we… we're going on another raid. The chief has promised me the antidote for you, if… if I fly well."

Wentworth moved heavily to the bars. Another raid!

"That's fine," he told Nita, hut his hand on hers was squeezing out a series of pressures in Morse code. *"Try escape,"* he signaled. *"I have plan."*

"Come, come, Nita," the chief said sharply, "you'll see him again in a few hours."

Nita turned away and hurried off with the procession. Wentworth waited until they had advanced a dozen yards then made the low throat sound which the Blanco had used to call the ape. There was a renewed shrill chatter and, abruptly, a small white shape was scampering along the tunnel. A whip cracked loudly, but the ape dodged and sprang, trembling, into Wentworth's

103

arms. The Blanco came—blundering back after him, and Wentworth got a firm grip in the ape's collar and waited.

The Blanco's face was twisted in rage. "You steal Con's ape!" the man growled. "Con kill you!" He shook the bars savagely.

"Get the keys," Wentworth whispered. "Unlock cell. Then Con can kill me and get ape! Don't let big boss know!"

"Con kill you!" the Blanco screamed, then a whip flicked out and cracked across his back. The Blanco cringed away from the bars, began to slink after the procession in response to a rasped order.

Wentworth waited, gripping the ape's collar. He stroked the chattering animal and, presently, it was quiet—the light fading from the corridor. Would his plan work? To accomplish it, the Blanco, Con, must escape from the procession and steal the keys from the guard....

Wentworth shook his head, frowning, but it was his one chance. He tied the ape to his chains with the shreds of the cloth about his waist and began more furiously than ever to scrub the link on the sand. Time dragged on, and nothing happened. IT WAS when Wentworth had almost despaired that the ape began to stir uneasily and utter a plaintive whimper. Wentworth drew it close and strained his eyes against the darkness. He choked back a groan. He could see the bars of his cage! Dimly, but unmistakably, he made out the bars. He could see in the dark! The implication of that discovery was maddening, but if he could escape now he might destroy the Blanco chief before he, himself, was bestialized. After that... well, a man must die sometime!

Presently, he made out the white loom of the beast-man beyond the bars.

"I am Dick," Wentworth growled, Blanco-fashion. "Dick killed Jed, who was the strongest man in the world. Dick is the strongest man in the world—the mightiest fighter!"

From the corridor, Con snarled back, "Con will kill Dick!"

Wentworth let silence fall between them, listening frantically—and then heard the chink of metal on metal. The Blanco had the key! Wentworth grew taut with eagerness.

"Con give Dick key," Wentworth said softly. "Dick give Con ape. We are two strong men. Why should we fight?"

The door swung open, and the Blanco slunk into the cell. If he attacked, Wentworth's chains would doom him! Wentworth freed the ape, and it fled chattering into the corridor. Con darted from the cell in pursuit—and left the cell door open! Almost unable to believe his senses, Wentworth groped his way heavily forward. From the lock dangled a ring of keys!

Swiftly, Wentworth stepped out into the corridor and hurried toward the cages in which Ram Singh and the others were imprisoned. At any moment, he might hear the alarm which would signal discovery of the theft of the keys, of his own escape.

Through the half-seen dimness of the tunnel, Wentworth groped his way until he could make out the vague shimmer of steel bars.

"Ram Singh?" he called cautiously.

"*Sahib!*" The Sikh gasped his reply, then laughed harshly. "Did I not say to you of weak heart that the master would find a way!"

Wentworth was already busy with the keys. He heard Janet

Rand begin to sob softly and the reassuring murmur of Dawson's voice. "Be quiet," he directed shortly. "My escape may be discovered at any moment."

His words cut off all talk as if a soundproof door had been shut. In the silence, the rasping of the key in its lock was very loud, and Ram Singh groped toward him, carrying his hampering chains.

"Do you know anything at all about this cavern or the guards?" he asked softly, as once more he sought the key to the cell of Dawson and the girl.

"Very little," Dawson said slowly. "We were brought straight to these cells. I know we came in a narrow entrance, through a chamber and into another tunnel. There was another big chamber and then this tunnel."

Abruptly, Wentworth hushed him. His listening ears had caught the sound of soft-padding feet coming rapidly along the corridor. There was no light. That meant those who approached were Blancos who could see in the dark!

"Dawson," Wentworth snapped, "take Janet and retreat along this corridor. Try to find weapons of some sort. I'll follow at the first opportunity. Ram Singh…."

"Han, sahib!" The Sikh was at his elbow. "Try your strength on this chain of mine," Wentworth said calmly. "I have weakened this link." Ram Singh's chained hands found the link, and Wentworth arranged the shackles so that all the strain would fall on the thinned portion of the iron. He set his shoulder inside the steel grating, braced himself.

"Now, *pull!*" he whispered. Instantly, Ram Singh's full weight

106

was thrown upon the chain. Wentworth gripped the links with his own hands and added his strength to the struggle. He heard a wailing, echoing cry burst out and knew that his escape had been discovered! The Blancos were within a few score yards.

"*Pull!*" Wentworth hissed. His own muscles were cracking under the strain. He could hear Ram Singh's panting breath, and the chains cut cruelly into his flesh. But still the weakened link did not give!

"Jerk!" Wentworth commanded calmly. "Stand as straight as you can, then throw yourself backward."

The footsteps were beating rapidly toward them. Almost, his sensitized eyes could make out the moving shadows that were the charging Blancos! The strain on the chain relaxed for an instant. Wentworth braced himself, then almost cried out with pain as Ram Singh hurled himself backward. Flesh was gashed on his wrists, but he wrenched violently. It seemed to him that something gave a slightest fraction of an inch. Yet still the chains held—and now there was no mistake about the Blancos! He could see their hulking shadows.

"Once more, Ram Singh!" he gasped. "Quickly or it will be too late!"

Ram Singh flung himself into the task. Once more, the manacles jerked taut, gouging into his wrists. There was an instant when the link still held and then—Ram Singh pitched to the earth and Wentworth staggered backward! He was partly free. The link he had severed was the key ring of the chain between his wrists, to which was also fastened the short length that stretched to his ankles. By severing that link, he had parted his hands, though lengths of chain still dangled from each wrist. He could now stand erect. His ankles still were linked, but, by comparison, Wentworth felt liberated—as if he had sprouted wings!

"Hold, fools!" he snarled, thickening his voice like a Blanco. "I am Dick. I killed Jed. I am the strongest man in the world!" **THE BLANCOS** checked their rush, crouched in the shadows. Wentworth could see vaguely now that there were three of them, and that each carried one of the villainous knives in his right hand.

"Throw down your knives," Wentworth snarled, "or I will kill you all!"

He took two hampered strides forward. He had no weapon save the footlong chain fastened to each wrist. He gripped those across his palms, swung them gently.

"Throw down your knives!" he commanded again.

Two of the Blancos retreated a step, but the third straightened to meet the challenge, and Wentworth saw that once more it was a case of leader battling leader, himself against this beast-man with his knife. Without a sound, Wentworth hurled himself forward, leaping with both chained feet together like a broadjumper, and as he sprang he struck with the two lengths of chain. One chain slashed viciously at the Blanco's face, the other met the sweeping stroke of the knife. Both blows went home!

The Blanco screamed terribly, one eye torn out, his right wrist broken—and Wentworth snatched the knife as it dropped. The Blanco's left hand darted for his throat, and Wentworth scarcely bothered to counter that attack. He let the Blanco come in and then struck with the knife—a swinging thrust at the back of the neck. He felt the blade drive home, but that crushing left hand closed on his throat with boa constrictor strength!

The Blanco was dead. No creature could live with the spinal column severed at the base of the brain—as Wentworth had done with that knife stroke. Yet that hand still clenched tighter upon Wentworth's throat. Wentworth went down under the rushing weight of the body, writhed and twisted aside, began to strike at the arm that was killing him. Two, three times the blade bit into flesh before the fingers loosened their awful hold and Wentworth staggered to his feet, more than half-unconscious, his lungs pumping.

Out through his torn throat, he forced the Blanco scream of triumph.

"Dick!" he cried hoarsely. "Dick is the strongest man in the world!"

Even while he shouted, it seemed a nightmarish thing—this struggle in the dark. He, a civilized man, a wealthy cosmopolite, triumphing over a beast-man in the darkness. Yet in his breast was a fierce eagerness for more battle! He realized that, and it shook him as not even the discovery of his escape had done. He could see in the darkness, and now he gloried in bloody, hand-to-hand battle! He mocked himself. By the heavens, he must hurry!

Neither of the remaining Blancos challenged his shout, and Wentworth growled at them. "Dogs," he said, "you are my men! If you do not obey, I will kill you!"

The men snarled, but it was submission.

Wentworth turned to Ram Singh. "This knife is like a small ax," he said, "and the iron of your fetters is soft. Hold your feet wide apart."

Three hacking blows sliced through a link and afterward, Wentworth cut the wrist chains the same way. Now Ram Singh could sever Wentworth's foot chains.

"Go ahead of me, Ram Singh," Wentworth directed then. "Find Dawson and the girl. There are many things to be done!"

"Han, sahib!" Ram Singh muttered, and Wentworth saw him grope his way along the tunnel, blindly. His chains made faint, metallic music. Wentworth turned on the conquered Blancos, bustled them into the cages and locked the door. He took their knives and followed Ram Singh.

Presently, he came upon Dawson and Janet Rand, huddled against the tunnel wall.

"Just ahead," Dawson said, "there is a steel doorway. There are no guards, but we couldn't get past it."

Wentworth thrust a knife impatiently into his groping hand, went swiftly to the steel door and fumbled with the keys. Unlike the other doors he had seen, this one was solid steel. There might be guards beyond it, but Wentworth did not hesitate. Somewhere here, there must be those masks the false Blancos had worn. If he could find them and whips, he could rally what Blancos were left against their own masters! Then, truly, he could lay a trap for the chief!

He found the key that fitted the door, turned the lock but eased it open, slowly. A thread of light sliced out into the pitch darkness and, for long moments, it dazzled Wentworth's eyes.

Then he could make out the scene beyond. Bent over a laboratory bench was a chubby, bald-headed man who wore thick glasses. As Wentworth watched him, the man poured a thick, greenish liquid into a sterilized bottle and began to seal it with wax. Wentworth kicked open the door and sprang forward. Behind, he heard Janet Rand gasp.

"It's Hans Lieberling!" she cried.

The man swung about, still clutching the bottle in his hand, and, as he turned, a deep bell began an infernal clamor off in the corridors of the cavern. Wentworth did not need to be told what that meant! By his invasion of the laboratory, he had set off alarms all over the stronghold of the Blancos. Within minutes, he could expect an avalanche of murderous guards upon his back!

CHAPTER 11
THE TRAP THAT FAILED

IN A long bound, Wentworth was upon the ruddy-faced scientist and had the blade of the Blanco knife against his throat. "Stop that alarm!" he ordered fiercely.

The blood drained from Hans Lieberling's face. "Plizz," he whispered. "Plizz, I do not know how it to stop!"

Wentworth swore savagely. He was constrained to believe the man because of his obvious terror. He darted back to the door, scanned the wall about it. His knife struck out and severed a cluster of wires. There was a bluish-white flash and the lights went out; the bells ceased to ring.

"Stand still, Lieberling!" Wentworth ordered, as he spun back toward the man. "I can see in the dark!"

"Himmel!" the scientist whimpered, "but I cannot!" From somewhere he produced a small flashlight and squeezed from it a narrow beam of light. It glittered on racks of test-tubes and retorts.

Wentworth snatched the flash from his hand and sent the light questing about. Three doors opened from the laboratory.

"Where do they lead?" Wentworth demanded.

Lieberling stammered that one led into another corridor; that one was a closet and the other gave on a cavern where men lived.

Instantly, Wentworth leaped to the closet. Dimly, he could hear the shouts of running men in the corridors. That steel door would stop them for a time, unless one of them also had the key.

At last, he fitted a key to the closet door and flung it wide open. A shout of triumph burst from his lips. Here were the masks he sought and bulky garments like the skins of the Blancos.

"Quickly, all of you!" he called. "Get into these things!"

He dragged suits from the walls and tossed them to the others, got down an armload of the casque-like masks and, inspecting one himself, he laughed. No wonder they were bulky and heavy! The suits included bullet-proof vests and the head-pieces were of steel....

Moments later, when Wentworth swung open the door of the laboratory, they were all, save Lieberling, encased in the disguising and protective garments. At their waists were strapped heavy automatics and, in their fists, they carried long-lashed whips.

Long-barreled flashlights threw bright white light ahead of them. They were ready now for the guard, but, at the door of the laboratory Wentworth hesitated.

"Lieberling," he said steadily "you have just one chance to live through this day. Obey orders implicitly, understand?"

"Ja wohl!" Lieberling chattered. "Ach, Gott, yes!"

"I understand, there is an antidote for this fluid that makes Blancos. Get a quantity of it."

Lieberling's face quivered with fear. "Ach, that I cannot do! There iss an antidote, but only one man could tell you—Doctor Rand. And him I have not seen since I came here."

"He is the chief?" Wentworth asked softly.

Lieberling nodded energetically. "So I think. I do not know. I come with the Blancos, to study them, then I a prisoner am made and forced to work in this laboratory. It iss interesting, but I would like better the Blancos to study."

For a long minute, Wentworth gazed into Lieberling's face, then he shrugged. He could not doubt that the man spoke truth.

"Forward!" he ordered grimly.

IF DR. RAND alone knew the secret of the antidote and Rand was the chief, Wentworth was doomed. For Rand would part with that secret only on condition of his release and that was a deal Wentworth would never make—not after the infamies the man and his martyred beasts had committed. Wentworth fought to crowd the thought from his brain as he took the lead and strode forward along the corridor, back the way they had come. He was ready now to meet the Blancos, ready to set his trap for the chief when he should return from his raid. If he won, he might try again to learn the antidote. But meantime....

The pattering beat of many feet, the hoarse breath of running Blancos, reached his ears. Wentworth focused his powerful flashlight up the corridor and shouted a command.

"Halt!" he called. "It is the command of the chief!"

In the outermost rim of the light, men skidded to a halt and Wentworth swung the whip, sent the long lash flicking ahead.

"Back where you came from, dogs!" he thundered.

The Blancos cringed, snarling, from the lash and began a heavy-footed retreat before him. There was no sound except their grunted cries and the shuffle of feet, until the first steel gate was reached. Blancos with whips stood outside it and a glance, now that he knew the truth, showed Wentworth that they were disguised men. There were two of them and they gripped the bars, peering toward him.

"What happened?" one of them shouted hoarsely. "The alarms went off!"

"The fool doctor," Wentworth growled back at them. "He set it off by accident."

The men cursed and swung open the gate. In a stride, Wentworth was beside them and his gun leaped up.

"Throw up your hands!" he ordered sharply.

With a curse, one of the men grabbed for his automatic and Wentworth's gun spat lead—not at breast or head, but at the gap between bullet-proof vest and steel-helmet. The bullet sped true. The man died, writhing, and the Blancos fled with shrill, plaintive cries down the tunnel. The concussion of the blast was deafening and, when Wentworth turned, he found that the other guard had died, too—with Ram Singh's knife in his throat!

"Quickly!" Wentworth snapped. "The second gate!"

Headlong, they fled down the corridor. Guns began to boom and Blanco screams shrilled out, but, before they reached the barrier, the battle was over. One dead Blanco lay in the middle of the corridor, the gate was ripped from its hinges and the guards had been literally torn apart.

The first cavern they reached was empty. Apparently, the men there had been transmuted into Blancos and freed. Wentworth hurried on, and they found the corridor that linked them with the outer chamber and the world outside. Here, too, the gate had been ripped open and, in the vaulted cavern, several score of Blancos milled excitedly. Wentworth swung the whip and made the lash crack like a shot.

"I am Dick!" he thundered. "I am the strongest man in the world! I am your new chief! When the old chief returns, we will kill him!"

A few men screamed challengingly, but they huddled together in little groups and kept wary eyes on the whips. Wentworth felt a huge relief settle upon him. He realized why the Blancos had not burst out into the outer world and freedom. Daylight shone at the exit.

WENTWORTH'S EYES blinked painfully at the sight of it, but it seemed to him that his whole soul hungered for sunshine, for one more glimpse of the world outside. He could not allow himself even a moment's rest. If it was daylight, the chief would be returning before long.

"How are the Blancos brought back to the cave?" Wentworth demanded of Lieberling. He waited with impatience.

The man shook his head. "They do not come back," he said sadly. "Herr Doktor Rand leaves them to kill until they are killed. But it does not bother him. Always, he says, he can make more and more."

Wentworth swore softly. That would prevent any outside force following the Blancos back, but it had a decided advantage for his plan. It meant the chief would return with only his bodyguard of whip-men. If he made a sudden, overwhelming attack....

"When I fire a shot outside," Wentworth said swiftly, "you will drive these men to the attack with your whips. Dawson, you take the party on the right. Ram Singh, you the one on the left. Stay behind and drive them into the force of whip-men. I'll pick out a few men and lie in ambush outside and, together, we'll wipe them out!"

Already, among the Blancos, Wentworth had spotted the one called Con with the ape on his shoulder. While Ram Singh and Dawson organized the ambush Wentworth strode straight toward Con.

"I am Dick!" Wentworth snarled.

"The ape is Con's!" the man grumbled back, cringing. "He has always been Con's."

"Keep the ape," Wentworth told him. "Get ten men and come with me." He held out an extra whip, snatched from a dead guard.

Con straightened slowly, and his lips grinned back from his

teeth. He took the whip and let it run through his fingers. With a hoarse scream, he whirled on the other Blancos and set about the work Wentworth had given him.

In less than fifteen minutes, the ambush was set. In the shrubbery near the cave mouth, Wentworth hid the ten Blancos and Con, while Ram Singh and Dawson set their watch inside. Wentworth had brought Lieberling along, a prisoner, and put quick questions to the man.

Lieberling spoke eagerly. "The second injection is made right into the pineal gland," he said. "The first, I do not know, but I think in the throat. But it is not all glands. The blood iss thicker and I have heard them scream with pains in the head. Even a dozen die from thrombosis—clots in the bloodstream. This new race is not perfect, no."

Wentworth frowned. The pineal gland he knew had something to do with the pigmentation of the body. Pituitary over-activity had been known to coarsen and bestialize adults.

"Thinning the blood, then," he said slowly, "might help to clarify the brains of some of the Blancos."

"*Ja!*" Lieberling agreed promptly. "But what to do about those glands, I do not know. No man knows—only Doktor Rand. I think, perhaps, many men died under the injections, *ja!*"

Wentworth studied Lieberling through eyes squinted painfully even in this shadowed light of the woods. Was the man lying? Was he actually the brain behind all this horror, cleverly perpetrating a hoax while he knew himself helpless?

Abruptly, Wentworth's head whipped up. Overhead, he caught the faint murmur of airplane engines. He uttered a low, mournful cry, heard Ram Singh answer and knew that the ambush was set. Was Nita with those returning planes, or had she made good her escape as he had bidden her?

Abruptly, Wentworth whirled on Lieberling and thrust a gag into his mouth. It was the work of moments, then, to bind him hand and foot. He glanced over the Blancos about him, the nearest the powerfully thewed Con with the ape on his shoulder. The ape was dangerous, but any attempt to displace him would precipitate a quarrel with Con, and he must have the Blancos' help.

"Soon old chief come," Wentworth whispered. "We kill! Then we both be chiefs!"

Con's lips snarled back from his teeth. "Con kill them all!"

"Con take other men to help," Wentworth directed.

Con muttered an assent, grumbled at the other Blancos crouched about him. Then Wentworth ordered silence, for the last motor had died and, already, he could her the dim beat of feet upon the trail.

Nothing would be done until the party had filed into the narrow mouth of the cavern, then he would lead a charge and his shot would precipitate an attack from within. Nita, he would make his personal task—the rescue of Nita and the death of the chief!

THE SOUND of voices reached his ears now, and he could make out the figures of the advancing party—twenty men with Nita and the chief in their midst. Wentworth swore under his breath. He had not anticipated so large a force. Too late to change his plans.

Wentworth rested a hand on Con's shoulder, felt the man's quivering eagerness. The ape perched there stirred restlessly. The party was abreast now, filing into the clearing before the cave mouth, and Wentworth's heart ached at the weariness in the carriage of Nita's brave shoulders.

Now the whole force was within the clearing, the leaders less than a dozen paces from the cave's mouth. Wentworth eased tensely into a crouch. In the next few minutes, he must triumph or fail. If he failed, the nation's thousands failed in that same instant, foredoomed before the onslaughts of the beast-men. In moments....

Without warning, the ape leaped from Con's shoulder and romped over the ground toward the chief's party. It raised a shrilled chattering that whirled every man in his tracks, hands leaping to guns. Wentworth's hand darted to Con—too late. With a hoarse cry, the beast-man rushed forward after his pet and, at the same moment, the whole group of Blancos charged!

The trap had been sprung too soon, and all the advantage was with the chief and his compact heavily armed force!

CHAPTER 12
FIGHTING CHANCE

WENTWORTH'S GUN leaped to his hand and he sprang forward in the wake of the charging Blancos. Before he could fire at the chief, the man had thrown an arm about Nita and dragged her body between himself and the attacking horde. A hoarse curse burst from Wentworth's lips.

More and more of the Blancos crowded into the car to wreak their havoc!

He fired point-blank into the nearest of the chief's men and, at the signal, heard the screams of the Blancos within the cave as they, too, joined in the rush.

Hope gushed into Wentworth's heart. Perhaps all was not lost! If the Blancos pressed the charge home from both sides... But the chief had caught the cries from within. His rasping voice rose in an order and, an instant later, the whole group was fighting an orderly retreat toward a narrow trail that climbed the cliff face. Con's Blancos had torn down several of the enemy, but the lashing whips cowed them. Wentworth plunged into the shrubbery and made a swift circling movement. He knew he could not reach the cliff-trail ahead of the others, but if he could reach the chief and Nita....

He peered out through the trees again and his lips thinned. The Blancos were sweeping out of the cavern mouth—but no farther. They huddled helplessly together, blinded by daylight, awed by the unfamiliar aspect of a sun-lit world. Instead of crashing the attack home, they fell to fighting among themselves as those in the lead sought to get back into the welcome darkness!

Wentworth swore raggedly. Without them, his attack was lost. For a wild moment, he considered a rush to rally them, but, even if they would follow him, there was no time. The chief, himself, was very close to that cliff trail which must take him out of reach. The chief was the crux of the battle. If Wentworth could reach him....

But the man kept himself well protected. He remained in the midst of his men and Nita formed a living shield despite her struggles. In a few moments, he would reach the foot of the trail. Once he started up that narrow path with Nita, Wentworth would not dare to shoot him lest, falling, he dragged Nita over the edge to her death!

Rage greater than any Wentworth had ever known began to pump through his body. With a scream, he hurled himself into the mêlée—and his shout was the tearing, rallying cry of the Blancos!

Two of the chief's men swung toward him with their whips. The lashes cut across his armored chest, clattered on the steel helmet. Wentworth laughed crazily and threw a careful shot in between the first man's helmet and corselet. Dying, he pitched back upon his fellows. A gun blasted, and Wentworth felt the kick of heavy lead against his chest protector. He stumbled, charged on, drove bodily into the close-packed circle of men before the chief. Two of them went down.

Behind him, Wentworth heard suddenly the berserk screams of attacking Blancos! Had some of them, then, answered his cry? He did not turn to see, but pushed on with renewed strength toward the chief and Nita! His rage was coldly terrible. The gun in his hand spat at point-blank range and bowled men from his path.

Only two remained now to block his way to the chief! The leader was running, backward, toward the trail. Nita's feet were clear of the ground, kicking futilely at his shins. With a shout, Wentworth sprang forward. Lashes licked out from behind him, tangled about his throat. Horses could not have held him back now. The gun slammed in his hand and the last two men who separated him from his prey went down. At the same moment, Nita lifted her feet high to drive backward at the chief's knees and, on the instant, Wentworth saw his opportunity. He drew a quick bead on the chief's ankles and squeezed the trigger... his gun clicked emptily!

THE CHIEF'S gun seemed to explode into his face, and Wentworth went down with lights flashing dazzlingly inside his skull. He wasn't hurt—just a blow on the helmet. He was up, instantly he thought—and yet the chief was now twenty feet above him on the cliff-trail. He no longer carried Nita in his arms, but dragged her behind him by the wrist, an effective cover for attack from the rear.

Wentworth angled away from the cliff base, stuffing cartridges into his automatic's clip. All around him were the sounds of battle. He blundered against fighting men, tore himself free from the coiled grip of a whip. He had eyes alone for those two figures scaling the cliff. He could see them only blearily because of his weakened eyes, but another thing grabbed his attention.

Not a half dozen feet above the chief was the mouth of a small cave! Once he reached that, he would be safe from all attack. Without a doubt, it connected somehow with the main system of tunnels within. Wentworth threw up his automatic to take careful aim. His eyes squinted painfully. God, he could not kill the chief! If he did, that grip on Nita's arm would drag her over the edge to almost certain death on the rocks below!

Only one thing to do... and his aim was far from sure! He must first smash a bullet through the arm whose hand held Nita a prisoner! There was no time to lose. He threw the gun in line, squeezed the trigger—and Nita pitched backward, arms flung wide, a scream on her lips! She stumbled, fell and half her body dangled over the void!

A mad cry surged to Wentworth's lips. For a crazed instant, he thought that his bullet had struck her. Then he realized she had been straining backward against that grip on her wrist and the sudden release had thrown her off balance. She was fighting to get a knee over the ledge, to climb back to safety. Then the chief... Wentworth's blurred eyes saw that the blow of lead against his wrist had twisted the man awkwardly against the cliff-face, spread-eagled him there for an instant, clear target for Wentworth's lead.

Triumph burning in his soul, Wentworth threw up his gun. He fired—but the chief was not there! He had delayed too long and the bullet only splintered rock dust from the cliff. The chief had flung himself prone into the mouth of the cave! Shouting curses, Wentworth sprang for the hill-trail, took great leaps up the narrow path—and for the first time in long minutes realized what was happening in the clearing before the cave.

The Blancos were fleeing wildly into the underbrush and, grouped close about the cave-mouth, were a half hundred whip-armed men. From some fastness where they had hidden and awaited opportunity, they had burst forth. Whips were not their only weapons—fully a dozen of them carried submachine guns! They wrought terrible havoc among the beast-men. Some of them were still charging. A few of the whip-men had been dragged down, but even the incredible stamina of the Blancos was not proof against the streams of .45 caliber slugs which literally chewed their bodies in half! Wentworth saw Ram Singh draw Dawson and Janet Rand to cover in the woods....

Wentworth ducked, as a bullet whined near his head. He realized the chief, still invisible above, had opened fire on him. It would be impossible to climb the trail in the face of such a barrage and, within moments, the men below would have cleared the field of Blancos, be ready to support the chief. He would be cut to pieces by a concentration of lead.

"Nita!" Wentworth called softly. "Hurry to me! We must escape!"

NITA HAD just managed to drag herself back to the shelf of the trail and lay there, panting. At Wentworth's call, she stared down incredulously at him in the disguise of a Blanco, then, with a glad cry, sprang to her feet and ran toward him. Above her head, Wentworth swept lead over the verge of the cave-shelf where the chief lay. He temporarily halted bullets from that point, but, within moments, knew the machine guns would turn his way.

"Faster, Nita!" he cried.

Nita hurled herself almost headlong down the trail. Once she stumbled and almost pitched out into space. A moment later, she bolted into Wentworth's arms. He caught her from her feet and leaped to earth. Wild shouts rang out behind. About his feet, as he sprinted for the trees, machine-gun bullets spewed up spats of white dust. Then he dived into the woods, took shelter behind the thick bole of a tree.

"Get to the planes," Wentworth told Nita swiftly.

Nita clung to him, "Thank God you got free, Dick," Nita

whispered. "I—almost made a break for it, and left you behind. Tonight, the beast-men are marching on New York!"

Wentworth gripped Nita by the shoulders. "New York!" he gasped. "Has the man gone mad?" A picture of the vast city, its unarmed, helpless millions ravished by the beast-men, sprang up before his eyes. Something very like a groan parted his lips. Back in the clearing the sounds of battle were dying out. Wentworth thrust horror from his soul. His course was obvious.

"Get to the planes," he repeated. "I'll send Dawson and the girl to you. Disable all the ships except one. Make sure it has a full load of fuel and be ready to take off."

Nita's hand clung to his arm. "But you, Dick?"

Wentworth tried to thrust her on her way. "I'll be there!" he snapped. "But if the other Blancos show first, take off! I may have to make my way through the woods...."

Nita clung to his arms. "I won't go, Dick!" she cried. "I won't!"

Wentworth caught her close for a moment. "You're ruining what small chances we have, dear," he said quietly. "New York must be warned. Cruising bomb planes might stop them on the roads. Now, hurry!"

Without waiting to see her start, Wentworth plunged into the trees. Nita's voice winged after him.

"Come to me—Dick, I'll wait!" she called.

Wentworth flung up a hand in acknowledgment and hurried on. He uttered a low wailing cry which Ram Singh would recognize, and the answer came softly from a score of feet ahead. In the clearing, the force of armored men was forming into compact groups. He could not see the chief, but heard his orders crackling. Wentworth could see Ram Singh and the others now.

"Dawson, Janet," Wentworth whispered, "take Doctor Lieberling. You'll find him tied up to the right of the trail, a dozen feet farther on. Go to the flying field below. Nita is there and will fly you to safety. We'll hold the trail."

Dawson shook his head. "We'll all go!" he said. "You got us out of there and we're not going to desert now…."

"Obey, fool!" Wentworth snapped, "or shall I send Ram Singh with you to see that you do!"

Dawson's eyes, through the slits of his mask, glittered angrily, and he gestured dissent.

"I'm going to join you, presently," Wentworth said impatiently. "Now hurry!"

Dawson crawled reluctantly away through the bush, and Janet followed.

Ram Singh settled himself on his belly behind an up-jutting boulder. "*Wah*, master," he cried softly, "it is like the olden times. We will slaughter these fools!"

A SMILE touched Wentworth's lips. He longed to send Ram Singh on his way, but he knew the Sikh would not obey now. As

128

for himself... Wentworth coolly sorted out ammunition from the pouch of the strange disguise he wore. Twenty cartridges and three—possibly four—in the automatic. Enough to make a very fair showing if the machine guns didn't get him first. He was still intent on getting the chief. What happened to him afterward did not matter greatly. Now that the battle rage had left him, he was remembering bitterly the beast-like fury of his charge. The Blanco was coming out in him more and more strongly, and there was no antidote....

A whimpering in the near-by brush jerked his head about and he saw the Blanco, Con, crouched there. There was a jagged tear in one shoulder where bullets had struck, but that was not the reason for his grief. He held the small white ape huddled against his chest—and the ape was dead. Wentworth frowned, then slowly his eyes narrowed in thought. That attachment between man and beast was a strange thing to develop so quickly. It seemed almost....

"Look, *sahib*," Ram Singh whispered, "an autogiro rises from the top of the cliff!"

Wentworth stared upward, and a curse leapt to his lips. The chief had not waited then for the outcome of the battle! With some one of his pilots, he had taken to safety in flight—and would hasten on to press his attack against New York! Wentworth's gun whipped up, but realized it was useless. His eyes shifted to the men formed up against the cliff. As he glanced that way, four, carrying machine guns, started toward the mouth of the trail and the others, in double file behind them, moved forward.

"The throat, Ram Singh," Wentworth called softly. "The four machine gunners first. Ready, aim… *fire!*"

At his word, their two automatics spoke and two machine gunners fell. An instant later the next pair of men fell, also, before that deadly fire. From the double file behind them, revolvers and rifles blasted out. The woods were swept by a gale of bullets. Twigs and leaves rained down upon Wentworth. A bullet struck the rock behind which he lay and whined off into the distance.

Wentworth kept his head down but, as the firing continued, he knew the men were advancing under cover of their lead. It was well organized, perfectly executed. Unless he could stop the advance, the angle of fire would soon overreach the protective boulders, and find them. He eased his helmeted head out to one side of the boulder and began a careful, sniping fire. When he squeezed the trigger, a man dropped. But there were too many of them and he glimpsed a party that darted into the woods to outflank him.

"Fall back," he called to Ram Singh. "We've got to hold them until the *missie sahib* can take off!"

Ram Singh was in his element. He had been born to such guerrilla hill fighting as this. He stole off into the underbrush, and Wentworth followed his lead. Moments later, they opened a deadly flank fire on the group in the clearing and were away before the attack could swing that way.

Instantly, Ram Singh led to intercept the flanking band, A low hillock commanded a reach of half-open woods and, on that, Wentworth directed a stand. The ten men of the flanking party crept into view presently, traveling single-file. They looked like some page out of primeval history in their Blanco helmets and suits like Blancos—but they carried modern arms!

When the entire ten were in sight, Wentworth touched Ram Singh's shoulder, and together they opened a rapid, deadly fire. Four men fell in a second of time, and two more dropped as they scuttled to cover. One of those who fell carried a sub-machine gun. Wentworth crept toward it, caught it up and gestured Ram Singh on.

"Now, we can win," he cried. "Get the Blanco, Con, and take him to the landing field."

Ram Singh stiffened in protest, but Wentworth slapped the comfortably heavy stock of the machine gun. "This is the key to the situation. Hurry, I'll be just behind you!"

RAPIDLY, WENTWORTH darted off through the woods, seeking a vantage point. He found a rocky cairn from whose crest he could enfilade the trail and sweep long lanes of the woods. The machine gun had an oversize drum, a hundred rounds of ammunition—and the drum was full.

Presently, he saw Ram Singh slip through the trees with the Blanco, pause to signal with his arm. Wentworth reassured him with a soft call and settled down to wait.

It was not long. Almost before Ram Singh was lost to sight, men began to filter singly through the woods, darting from tree to tree. It was the one method of attack which Wentworth could not hope to combat successfully for long. Groups he could stop; he could spot many of the men who advanced singly but the rest would get by.

He waited until a dozen men were in sight, then began squeezing off short bursts. Five dropped, but the rest darted to cover and, from a half dozen different spots, lead began to sing toward him. Wentworth's lips curved in a harsh line. He had been prepared, at the battle's beginning, to sell his life for that of the chief, but that no longer was the issue. He must survive to reach, and remove the man who menaced the key city of the nation.

He kept to his concealment and fired only when he had a fair target, but the guns against him increased steadily. Bullets whined and hammered viciously around him. A slug glanced off his helmet and made his head sing—and still he had not heard the roar of Nita's plane taking off.

A bullet drove down at a sharp angle and struck between his shoulders, hammered the breath from him despite his bullet-proof protector. He swiveled the muzzle of his machine gun upward, but another bullet had hammered against his helmet before he dislodged the sniper from the tree where he had climbed. The machine gun was much lighter in his hands now, and he realized that many of the bullets had been fired. He could not hold out much longer. He spotted another sniper in a tree and got him through an arm so that the man pitched, screaming, to the ground.

Instantly, a heavy fire opened on him from the opposite direction. Wentworth whipped his machine gun around and blasted a clump of bushes—then the machine gun went dead. Empty! Wentworth dropped it and caught up his automatic. The battle was close to an end now. He counted his bullets—ten left! Should he make a break for the woods behind him, hope that he might dodge bullets from so many angles? It was no use. Better to stay here in hiding, hold them back as long as possible, and then… Well, there would be one Blanco fewer in the world.

Wentworth had never known such inhibiting despair. Tight situations had never before sapped his courage… Not that he would not fight to the last ditch, but the outcome no longer seemed important to him personally. Nita would carry the warning. Someone else would succeed where he had failed and wipe out the chief. Soon his own keen brain would be slowed by thickening Blanco blood….

Wentworth fought against an impulse to charge wildly into the few remaining guns. It would end it more quickly—but he must give Nita her full opportunity to escape. Once more the insensate rage that drove the Blancos to charge their enemies despite mortal wounds began to surge up through him. He closed his eyes and fought against the temptation. A sniper bullet from high up angled down at him and chipped a stone beside his head, but he did not stir. If he so much as moved, he felt that he would hurl himself down from his cairn and charge, charge *screaming*….

Abruptly, frenzied cries burst out in the near-by woods. There was a fresh and furious outbreak of firing, and Ram Singh's voice came to him clearly, calling in Punjabi.

"We are rolling up their flank! Flee, *sahib!* We rally at the airport!"

WENTWORTH OPENED his eyes and realized that the gunfire directed at himself had ceased. Men were taking cover against an attack upon their left flank, and a half dozen were exposed to his own gun. He hammered out a swift series of shots and the battle line broke. Men fled in panic back through the woods toward the cliff. Once more, Wentworth screamed in rage and leaped to the charge. He cleared the cairn in a long leap, hit running—and a man stepped into his path. Wentworth jerked up his gun. It snapped futilely, and then the man closed.

"*Sahib! Sahib!*" the man pleaded. "It is I—Ram Singh!"

Wentworth felt strong arms close about him, felt himself lifted and carried at a jogging, staggering run. His eyes closed. Presently, he aroused himself again.

"I'm all right now, Ram Singh," he said quietly.

He jumped to the ground, and they ran together. He realized that Nita was just ahead of him; that Dawson and Lieberling ran with guns in their hands. They had risked everything to come back and rescue him… to rescue a Blanco!

Wentworth thrust the thought from his brain. He still had a duty to fulfill, a mission to perform. When that was finished… But now he must take command.

"Nita, Dawson, Janet in one plane," he directed. "Nita, you will make all possible speed to New York. A phone call would be worse than useless. Ram Singh, Lieberling, get the Blanco into the other plane. Ram Singh, to the controls."

Wentworth pivoted and stared back into the woods. Doubtless, the men were reforming, but they would be too late.

Nita ran toward him. "I'm going with you, Dick. Ram Singh can pilot the other plane."

Wentworth shook his head.

"Dick, there are many things I have to tell you," she insisted.

Wentworth took her shoulders in his hands. "We have a few moments, dear," he said. "Speak rapidly. You'll have to go. Ram Singh would not be able to get through to the necessary officials."

Defiance was on Nita's face, but she began to talk swiftly as he ordered. "The loot has been carried eastward by plane," she said. "I don't know where. He already has his Blancos near New York. But there, again, I don't know where. I tried to get a plane into the air to follow the autogiro, but we had only a short load of fuel, and it wouldn't have helped. Dick, why can't we carry that warning together?"

Wentworth unfastened his casque and took it off. The light struck into his Blanco eyes and he had to squint in order to see Nita's face.

"I'm not going to New York," he said quietly, "unless I am unable to find the chief before that time. If I can destroy him, there will be no attack on New York."

Nita stepped back and looked pleadingly into his face, but there was unshakable resolve there. With a small sob, she flung herself against his chest, drew his lips down to hers—then ran to her plane. As she waved a hand from the cockpit, he was still standing there, as if he could not see her long enough, as if... as if he would never see her again. The hair on his head, the beard on his unshaven cheeks, was white as any Blanco's.

CHAPTER 13
THE GREY HORDE

NITA'S EYES were so dim with tears she nearly crashed her plane in that precarious take-off from the small hill-country flying field. She did not see the trees looming ahead of her until they were perilously near and, even then, it was more flying instinct than conscious skill which caused her to zoom over the up-reaching branches.

Her mind and heart had room only for that last glimpse of Wentworth—Dick, her Dick, with his hair white and those peering, weak eyes that were like a sick old man's. Yet she must leave him—as ever, in his extremity—to speed on some errand of the service in which he had pledged himself and which she, alone among woman-kind, knew. He needed her terribly now, more than ever before in his vigorous, aggressive life. Her woman's heart told her that.

It was with difficulty that Nita drove her mind back to the task. But it was vitally necessary. For moments after the take-off, the plane drove into thick, low-lying clouds now just beginning to creep across the sky. A new apprehension sprang up in her breast. How far did the cloud area stretch? In such weather, the lingering coldness of the sea, combined with the warm, humid air, could form impenetrable fogs along the eastern seaboard. Her plane was not equipped for blind landings. It had a radio receiving-set, but no sending-key. Sure trouble lay ahead, and behind her—Dick....

Nita's apprehensions of fog were more than fulfilled. When

136

she reached what she calculated to be the vicinity of New York, the entire coast was wrapped in dense mist. The weather broadcasts reported zero-zero—ceding zero, visibility zero—from Maine to Hatteras and as far west as Pittsburgh. For hours, she circled over the field to which the radio beacon led her, hoping for a window in the fog that would let her land. More than once, she was tempted to risk a blind landing, but the memory of near-by high-tension wires and factory chimneys stopped her.

It was not that she lacked the courage to risk death. She would have taken the chance gladly had Wentworth been beside her. But so much depended on her survival. It was not alone that Dick counted on her to carry the warning to New York City, to their friend, Stanley Kirkpatrick, commissioner of police. Nor was it exclusively the thought of the thousands who would die at the hands of the Blancos if the attack were not prevented. She was capable of altruistic sacrifice but she could not forget how desperately Dick needed her.

One thing she *could* do. She called to Dawson and Janet, seated in the enclosed cockpit behind her and finally made them understand that they must write notes of warning, signed with Wentworth's name, and drop them to the airport, weighted with tools or everything movable in the ship. There was a chance that someone would spot those down-fluttering messages and relay the word to Kirkpatrick. It was a feeble expedient, but the best she could contrive.

Finally, frantic over a dwindling gasoline supply, Nita was nerving herself to risk landing blind, when she caught the first message of hope. A liner reported itself a hundred miles off

Montauk lightship and lying-to outside the fog-belt. Nita's eyes jumped to the gas-gauge. If she could reach that ship, it would have a wireless telephone by which she could get through to Kirkpatrick. It meant a landing in the cold sea water, but a note dropped on the ship's deck would get a boat lowered in advance—if she could find the liner and if, meanwhile, the fog did not swallow it!

Nita's soft lips closed firmly. It was the one—the *only* chance. Within an hour, the darkness of the overcast skies would fall. After that, it would be too late to take even this wild risk. After that... the Blancos would strike! Without a moment's longer hesitation, Nita took her risk. She turned the plane's nose eastward and opened the throttle.

"Dick," she whispered. "Oh, Dick, for your sake, I must not fail!"

FAR AWAY to the westward, Wentworth's plane was winging its way swiftly toward New York. The same thick weather that had trapped Nita in the skies had foiled his already nearly hopeless search of the mountain fastnesses of the east on which he had fixed as the probable hiding-place of the chief and his loot. Since that chance of preventing the invasion of New York was lost, Wentworth had no choice save to speed there and join battle—to attempt, during the mêlée, or afterward, to pick up the trail that would lead him to the chief and destroy him.

Wentworth's plane was a small cabin job. He was wedged in beside Ram Singh, who still held the controls. Behind him, Hans Lieberling sat beside the wounded Blanco, whose powerful arms still cuddled the dead ape. Above the roar of the motor, Wentworth shouted to Lieberling.

"You believe thinning the blood may help clear a Blanco's mind," he cried.

Lieberling nodded, thick glasses glittering.

"When we land at New York," Wentworth shouted, "you will operate on this Blanco and thin his blood. It must be done quickly. He has been close to the chief and should be able to tell us something if we can restore him to normal intelligence."

He eyed Con and the dead ape, and the Blanco lifted his rheumy eyes pleadingly.

"I have a theory…" Wentworth began slowly. He chopped it short, faced forward to talk briefly with Ram Singh about their course. The weather broadcast was still zero-zero, and the loudness of the radio beacon proved they were drawing close to the airport.

"I'll take over," Wentworth said quietly. Ram Singh resigned the controls to his hands and Wentworth blinked down at the instruments. There was a question in his mind. His eyes were best suited now to darkness, and already early night had closed down on the earth below. What would the fog do to his vision? He did not know, but he had resolved upon a desperate venture if the fields were inaccessible because of fog.

Abruptly, the radio signals ceased and Wentworth peered downward. Not even a glimmer of the field lights, which he knew to be just beneath because of the silence of the radio, was visible. He nodded slowly to himself, returned until he located the exact point at which signals ceased, then swung deliberately toward New York City and the East River.

Wentworth was aware of Ram Singh's eyes peering at him fixedly, of the tension of Lieberling behind him. Wentworth's lips shut in a straight line.

"Ram Singh," he said quietly. "I am going to land in the East River. This plane will float for a few minutes. In that time you must get Doctor Lieberling clear. I'll take care of the Blanco. I'll land as near home as possible."

Wentworth spoke calmly, but no one realized better than he the slim chance of success in the venture. Four great bridges spanned the East River. Islands cluttered it and there would be tugs and shipping, but even so, Wentworth believed there was less risk there than in landing on the earth. A small crack-up would not be as dangerous, provided no one was knocked unconscious. That would be up to him.

Even while he spoke, Wentworth was cutting his altitude. He had headed due eastward after leaving the airport and, somewhere ahead, the lighted tower of the Empire State Building would be thrusting a fifth of a mile into the dense fog. Wentworth's altitude was already down to twelve hundred feet. He held it there—and prayed that the altimeter had been calibrated recently. If it were wrong, he might smack head-on into the very building he sought to guide him!

THROUGH THE night, he strained his eyes. The glow of a thousand lights, refracted by the mist, threw a roseate glow over the fog-clouds. He was gambling on the fact that his eyes were more sensitized to light than those of normal human beings. It was a gamble, but… Abruptly, Wentworth kicked the rudder savagely, threw the stick over violently, then straightened on his course again. Just clear of his wing-tips, the tower of the Empire State Building swept past and was immediately swallowed in the fog.

Wentworth's lips twitched in a slight smile. His theory was right, but the fog was thicker than he had realized. He was sweeping southward now toward the tip of Manhattan, curving eastward. Impossible to gauge distances exactly in the wool-thickness of fog, but somewhere below him must be the river shore. Deliberately he cut the motor and strained his ears, snapped open a section of the windshield so that the wetness of the night slid against his face. It roused him.

Then he caught the sounds he sought, the hoarse multiple whistles of the harbor—of the East River. Slowly he opened the throttle again, kept the nose of the ship down. He had cut his altitude to less than five hundred feet—less than four hundred. Once more, his eyes were straining seeking the red lights that would mark the topmost point of the bridges that spanned the river. He knew that his altimeter had an error of more than a hundred feet, for he had been below the top of the Empire State Building when he should have been above it, according to the altitude gauge.

Abruptly, Wentworth's breath gusted from his lungs. He jerked the throttle, pulled back on the stick and the gleaming black superstructure of a bridge, crested by red lights, skimmed by just beneath him. He had no more than a glimpse of it, but that was enough. Wentworth knew his Manhattan intimately, and he knew the structure of its bridges. It was the Williams-burg span.

Wentworth cut the motor again and drifted downward toward the breast of the river. His home, built partly upon filled land between two piers on the East River back of Sutton Place, was in the Fifties, about two miles upriver. He eyed his watch, made a shrewd guess at the flying speed.

"I'm landing in the river," he called to Lieberling. "Ram Singh will take care of you. Have you figured out a way to thin the Blanco's blood?"

"I have a plan," Lieberling began slowly.

"Good!" Wentworth snapped.

He leaned forward. He needed all his energies now. His altimeter was useless at this low height. His speed was barely sufficient to keep the plane in the air. His right hand crept to the throttle. His left joggled the stick to keep the wings level. Well he knew that the fate of the city flew with him. Even if Nita had got through with the warning—and he could not see how that would be possible in this fog—the police plans would only include fighting the Blancos. There would be no thought of capturing the chief. Wentworth felt that at last he had a clue—or the means of developing a lead that would point out to him the identity, if not the hiding-place, of the chief of the Blancos! He must survive until then....

A twinge touched his heart then, remembering Nita flying these inscrutable skies, fighting a fog that would defy the peak skill of fully experienced flyers. Nita was a natural, but her hours of flight did not total two hundred. Nita... Wentworth was not a man given to prayer, but there was in his heart a petition that the hands of some Providence would guide hers this night! For himself, once this night's battle was over, nothing much mattered. He was no longer a man, but a Blanco! Bitterness twisted his fine lips, and then he saw it, straight ahead, and towering upward like a cliff—the side of an anchored liner!

A shout of warning rose to Wentworth's lips. The plane could not gather speed quickly enough to hurdle the ship. Only one thing left to do—shove it down into the water and hope to stop before collision with that motionless steel side smashed the life from them.

Even in that crucial moment, Wentworth was thinking. He cut the ignition, dived, jerked the stick to slam the tail against the water first. He felt the tail catch the surface. The rest of the ship shuddered, whipped down as the landing-gear plucked at the water. The mountainous steel flank of the liner was just ahead. There came a thunderous, splashing crash. A man screamed....

NEW YORK'S millions were trooping homeward through the early night over streets greasy and wet with fog. The upper floors of even low buildings were swathed in mist. Streams of automobiles poured northward. Buses and street cars were crowded to the doors, but it was the subways that carried the bulk of the rush-hour load. Below the streets, concrete platforms were jammed thick with people, turnstiles made a continual clatter and train followed train so closely they formed an almost continuous chain.

If people felt any nervousness over the fact that, a week before, a horde of Blancos had invaded a subway, at least no one showed his apprehensions. It had been a single outbreak, quickly quelled, and there had been no fresh attack. True, several hundred people had been killed, but even such a catastrophe had been crowded off the front pages of newspapers—and New York lived by its newspapers. There had been no fresh developments in New York. Investigation had failed to discover the source from which the Blancos had sprung.

It was true that entire towns out in the Middle West somewhere had been almost destroyed by Blancos, but that was in Kentucky, or Tennessee—one of those funny, mountain states—and *this* was New York. Things like that just didn't happen in New York, the proud, busy city of spires and building giants! It never occurred to them that the first outbreak might be experimental, a test attack intended to point the way for the future and used, at the time, to divert attention from more lucrative, less hazardous western raids. Two hundred persons horribly murdered as an experiment? Too silly to think about!

Jammed into the first car, of a northbound express, by shouting guards, a girl smiled up at the man beside her, a co-worker in her office.

"It's silly," she called, above the clatter of the train, "but ever since those ape-men killed all those people, I feel nervous about riding the subway!"

The man smiled down. "Lean on my manly bosom," he said. "I'll protect you!"

People who heard, swaying as the train lurched and roared through the tunnels, smiled a little at the two, but traces of uneasiness touched their faces. A dapper man, wedged into a corner, shouted to another man.

"Police take care of things like that damned quick in this man's town. Things that happen out west couldn't happen here!"

The other man nodded. "No danger!"

No danger... but some people stared uneasily at the blur of steel roof-columns flashing past, at the dim lights of this man-made cavern beneath the city streets—so like those other caverns far away which housed horror. Stations sped by. People fought their way into the already jammed train. It slammed into Grand Central, lost some hundreds, picked up hundreds more, got under way with a hiss of released air, a moan of taxed motors.

"Almost home," the man shouted down at the girl. "Got anything to do tonight?"

"A million," the girl called up, "but I can't think of one!"

They smiled into each other's faces. They were pressed very close together in the crowd, and the man's hand closed on hers. They were still smiling when the train lurched heavily and the lights went out, leaving only the dim emergencies burning— when the steel coach ground against the close concrete walls of the tunnel and window glass flung its spearing shreds into the crowd. The dapper man was catapulted like a projectile through the crowd and a woman screamed, plucking at glass in her throat.

The boy flung his arms around the girl and fought against the already surging panic, and then his face went drained and grey. The front door of the car stood open and a figure was climbing through it, sheathed in grey—a grey raincoat that glistened with

145

the damp and, over his head, a grey hood with cutout holes for the eyes. A powerful arm swept upward and a knife glittered in the dim light as it swept down... rose and fell again. It glittered no longer, but shone dully, coated in red. A man, frantic with fear, grabbed wildly at the figure and the hood tore loose before the man died, terribly.

It was then the boy screamed and the girl's piercing cry rose, high and wild, into the night, for they saw the face of the thing with the knife, and it was not the face of a human being. It was the face of a beast—a Blanco ape-man!

Their cries were lost in the bedlam of shouts and screams that burst from the thousands jammed into the train as they realized the full hopelessness of their position. Crowded so closely together they could scarcely lift a hand in self-defense, unarmed, they fought to escape backward through the train. Men and women went down underfoot, were trampled—and behind them was horror. For reinforcements of Blancos crowded in to wreak their fearful carnage. Their triumphant, blood-lusting screams pierced far beyond the others. The knives rose and fell. A woman was snatched up by the hair and a clawing hand ripped her naked in an instant. A man charged in mad panic, and a knife struck with the sound of a cleaver driving into a joint of beef.

IT WAS long before the alarm reached the surface and the ears of the tautly ready police. Not until people had burst from the rear of the beleaguered train and run, screaming, to the trains behind, stopped by signal blocks; not until the motorman had grasped the hell that had broken loose ahead and went racing to emergency telephones! Then the radio-broadcast station at headquarters went crazy; emergency wagons shrieked through the streets and heavily armed men leaped into waiting automobiles to speed to the rescue.

Nita's warning had got through, a penciled note snatched from the mud of Newark airport. But what could they do against madmen whom only a deluge of bullets could halt—and that often too late? What could they do when the crazed, frantic reports of slaughter came from a dozen scattered spots in the city where subway trains had been wrecked, where thousands were being slaughtered by beasts—men who screamed and dipped their fanged mouths in blood!

Through the streets raced a heavy, black car in which two men sat tensely, one of them with his dark, bearded head bound in a white turban. The other man squinted with pain-filled eyes, his whitened hair hidden beneath a broad-brimmed black hat, his slouching body that had once been so erect sheathed in a long black cape. Ram Singh and his master were rushing into battle, too, and for this battle Wentworth had chosen to wear the garb that had won honor on so many criminal battlefields—the garb of the Spider!

In Wentworth's heart was a dread that this might be his last battle—and it was not all dread. From Kirkpatrick, he had learned that Nita's message had come from the air, and he knew what that meant. She had not been able to maneuver a landing—trapped in the skies until her gasoline gave out, and then....

Wentworth shuddered away from the impact of that thought, and it seemed to him that he and all his loved ones had reached the end of the long road. It had begun so trivially back there in the Kentucky hills with the disappearance of a few scarcely missed men, and now…Wentworth thrust the thought from his brain. He had barely made his contact with Kirkpatrick, after they had been fished from the sinking plane by men from the liner, when the horror had struck.

Wentworth had given a few brief advices, drawn from his own pain. Blinding lights would be the best weapons against the Blancos—bright lights and whips. Machine guns might stop them, but only after fearful carnage.

"I'm going into the fight, Kirk," he finished quietly. "If I don't come back, there's a Blanco at my home who may be in condition to talk after the surgeon gets through with him. I think he can tell you the name of the leader of this murderous horde."

Kirkpatrick had said wonderingly, "Your voice sounds funny, Dick—hoarse, scarcely recognizable."

Wentworth had laughed bitterly and hung up. Yes, his voice was strange, as his face and his body were strange—as the brain which drove him mercilessly to the task he had set seemed scarcely his own. For it worked out fumblingly the things that it should decide in a flash. As he crouched now beside Ram Singh, he listened to radio calls to the police, telling of the slaughter beneath the streets and knew that there was something he should deduce from this subway attack—but could not find it out. He raised a gnarled hand to his face, and the hand trembled. He beat his forehead, slowly, heavily, with a clenched fist… Something he should be able to figure easily—and could not.

Abruptly, the announcer's voice broke out again. "A new

attack in the subways," it said clearly. "Lexington Avenue line, near Twenty-third Street Station."

Wentworth trained his eyes to catch a street sign flashing past, and the light blinded him.

"We should be near there, Ram Singh," he muttered. "Go there. We'll be before the police, and perhaps...."

"My master forgets," Ram Singh said quietly. "He wears the garb of the Spider!"

"Obey!" Wentworth shouted, and the fierce, hoarse voice, that was new to his throat, cracked with beast-like rage.

Ram Singh stiffened, "I hear and obey, master," he mumbled. For one moment, his eyes swung toward Wentworth and there was worship there, and a pity that was like knives.

Wentworth swore under his breath. Beneath his cape, he fumbled and brought forth two long-lashed whips.

"We fight with these," he said.

Ram Singh slued the car to a halt beside the Twenty-third Street kiosk. People were streaming from it madly, scream-ing in their terror, or running in white-faced, silent panic that blinded them to all else but the danger behind. Wentworth sprang quickly to the pavement.

"Ram Singh," he said, "report to Kirkpatrick. Tell him I believe fire may also frighten the Blancos."

Ram Singh stepped to the pavement beside Wentworth. "Master," he said, "I go with you!"

For an instant, Wentworth glared at him, the new and flick-ering rage hot in his breast.

"Fool!" Wentworth snarled. "I go to my death!"

"Han sahib!" Ram Singh acknowledged, still with his quiet calm.

A moment longer, Wentworth attempted to drive Ram Singh from him, then slowly his lips parted in something like his old smile. His fingers bit into Ram Singh's shoulder, then abruptly he turned and led the way down the steps up which the thousands fled blindly. It was a fight to reach the platform. After they had sprung to the road-bed, it was easier. The running fugitives told them the location of the train, and Wentworth headed for the scene of battle with his breath hot in his nostrils, the whip coiling and uncoiling in his restless hands.

WHEN FIRST he saw the Blancos in their grey garb, he checked for a moment, puzzled—then he understood and raced on. This was the way they had passed through the city streets. Easy to hide even a beast's body under that long grey coat. Probably the hoods had been added merely to lend a note of additional terror to their unveiling in battle. Wentworth threw back his head and screamed as he ran, screamed the rallying cry of the Blancos.

"To me, Blancos!" he shouted. "To me! I am Dick! I am the strongest man in the world! I will kill all who do not obey!"

Ahead of him, two Blancos were half through the windows of a train, hacking with bloody knives at the packed humanity within. At Wentworth's scream, they turned ferocious faces, snarled defiance. Wentworth's long-lashed whip struck out and ripped the rubber coats from their backs, dug into the flesh.

"Obey!" he screamed, "or I will kill you!"

The Blancos cringed and one dropped to the ground. Wentworth struck again and the second Blanco screamed in pain and crouched, whimpering like a dog.

"Obey!" Wentworth shouted. "Call the others here!"

Once more, Wentworth sent up his rallying call. He ran along the side of the train, and the whip slashed and cracked. Beside him ran Ram Singh and his whip, too, took heavy toll among the grey, creeping horde. Ahead, Blancos paused uncertainly in then fearful carnage. The crack of the whips brought terror to souls that bullets could not daunt.

In ten minutes of fearful work, Wentworth had gathered the Blancos into a tight huddle near the front end of the train. Twice he had emptied his automatic into Blancos who would not heed the whip, and one of them had nearly killed him. Only Ram Singh had saved his life by using the whip as a garrote and holding the Blanco until he died.

Now, as the last man was yielding, the police burst into the tunnel with blazing lights and blasting guns. Wentworth sprang toward them, both hands upraised.

"Stop, you fools!" he shouted. "I have them beaten!"

A man cried hoarsely. "Good God, the Spider!"

From somewhere in the thick, blue ranks, a pistol spoke and Wentworth felt a sledge blow drive him backward a full pace. He stood, swaying on his feet, and the old blind rage surged up through him. He screamed hoarsely, took a long stride forward… and something wrapped about his throat from behind and dragged tightly about his neck. His scream was choked off. He turned, dragging at his gun, and above him was Ram Singh's compassionate face. It was Ram Singh's whip that was strangling him, that was darkening all the world. Wentworth tried to get his gun out, but it was pinned against his side. The world blotted out of his consciousness....

CHAPTER 14
THE LAST DESPERATE STAND

THROUGH THE vague darkness that shrouded him, Wentworth was conscious of being carried, of a distant hubbub, shots. It seemed to him that his head was clearer than in days, that his mind was working... But there was a vital reason why he should recover and break the bonds of helplessness that held him. Something he should understand....

He opened his eyes as Ram Singh placed him in the car and sprang to the wheel, felt the cool rush of damp air upon his face. The fog made fast driving precarious, but Ram Singh hurled the car furiously through the streets. Wentworth again turned his attention upon the problem that beset him, and abruptly he sat up straight. A twinge of pain ran through his body, and he remembered he had been wounded... He ignored it.

"Ram Singh," he snapped, "get me back home at once."

Ram Singh's head twisted about, "You are wounded, master! Thy forgiveness for that I laid hands upon thee, master, but...."

"Forget it, Ram Singh," Wentworth ordered. "As for the wound, I am a Blanco, and Blancos do not bleed. Home, fast!"

The big car gathered speed, rushed northward through the city, skidded wildly on the curve as it swung finally into Sutton Place, turned right upon a dead end street whose left side was formed by a high, stone wall. Steel gates slid apart as the car charged them, clanged shut again behind. Wentworth sprang from the car, reeled and almost fell, but straightened resolutely and rushed into the house.

"Get the amphibian ready!" he shouted over his shoulder to Ram Singh.

He heard the beginning of a protest, no more. He had slammed himself into the elevator which shot him swiftly upward. Moments later, he rushed into the room where Con, the Blanco, lay upon a bed with Dr. Lieberling bending over him.

"What results?" Wentworth snapped.

Lieberling straightened jerkily, "I know who he is!" he said rapidly.

"Yes, yes," Wentworth said impatiently. "He's Doctor Conoly Rand. I guessed as much because of his attachment to the ape that had been Doctor Rand's pet. But what does he say about the chief?"

Lieberling shook his head, "He doesn't know the man's identity. He always wore a Blanco mask. I think…" Lieberling turned to the Blanco. "He's coming around again."

Wentworth bent over him, "Doctor Rand!" he called, harshly in his tension. "Doctor Rand—you must speak to me!"

The Blanco's eyes opened slowly. "Yes," he said thickly. "Yes, I am Doctor Rand!"

"Listen to me carefully," Wentworth said swiftly. "The attack on New York was a blind, wasn't it—intended to cover the chief's escape?"

Dr. Rand blinked up at Wentworth. "I think you are right,"

he said heavily. "That was the proposal that was made to me when I was kidnaped. He tried to make me help him, outlined a plan. Loot small cities—then attack a big city with all the Blancos left alive. Make an escape while that was done. If this is New York...."

"I am sure of it!" Wentworth said quickly. "All the attacks by the Blancos are in the subways. There has been no effort at looting. It's a smoke-screen. Now, tell me. How was he going to escape—and where?"

Rand's eyes closed heavily. His breathing was rapid, painful.

"Come, come!" Wentworth threw at him. "One more word, and you can rest! Where was he going?"

"I am trying... to remember," Rand said thickly. "Something about a plane. A big seaplane. He was going to steal one and fly out to sea. No one would ever find him again, he said."

Wentworth snapped erect, staring with burning eyes at the fog-banked window. A big seaplane, stolen... Only one place where he could get one that he would dare go to sea in—the Pan-American seaport for the Bermuda planes! By the heavens....

Wentworth reeled about, blundered against the facing as he went through the door. Dr. Lieberling ran after him.

"Are you wounded?" he demanded swiftly.

Wentworth brushed it aside, laughing fiercely, "Blancos don't bleed!"

THE ELEVATOR was waiting and he slammed in, dropped it straight down to the basement and below it into a secret tunnel way that led straight to his amphibian's hangar. He could hear the motor roaring and broke into a staggering run.

He was trying desperately to figure the time element. The chief had a half-hour's start by plane from the hideout in the Kentucky hills, but his autogiro plane would have been slower than their own ships. In the 'giro, especially if equipped with blind-landing devices, he would have been able to make a safe landing. Then, time to collect the loot, transport it to the Pan-American seaport, steal a plane....

Wentworth's breath began to come more quickly. With luck, he might yet be in time! He wavered toward the amphibian. Beyond it, the doors stood open and the fog banked up solidly. He could barely glimpse the water, Ram Singh hurried toward him.

"Master, this is madness," he pleaded.

Wentworth stepped close, and struck with a chopping punch to the point of the jaw. Ram Singh went down and out, and Wentworth ran to the plane, got into it and kicked off the brakes. The pull of the propeller drew it down the short slope and into the water. Moments later, the shore faded out behind him.

He yanked the throttle wide, running blind into the dense mists. Finally, the ship shook free of the water and lifted. Wentworth skimmed the funnels of a tug with only inches to spare and laughed wildly. His luck had turned, he felt. He would find and kill the chief, and then....

Wentworth's face puckered oddly, but no sound forced its way from between his tightened lips. He glanced at the compass and slanted for the Long Island airport of the Pan-American line. He felt a strange fatality about his movements. He had no doubts of his whereabouts at all when presently he cut the altitude, and it was with no sense of surprise that he spotted the red markers about an airport.

He cut the motor to idling speed, drifted downward... and heard the swift hammer of a machine gun! Even while he angled down, straining his eyes to see the scene below, he heard the heavy roar of multiple motors. Instantly, they began to move away.

Wentworth cursed. He had been just too late, but he could follow! He dropped lower and lower until he could make out the roar of those engines even above his own opened throttle. The big ship was headed due east. Wentworth's hands went with the familiarity of long practice to the breeches of the twin machine guns set in the forward cowling. They were hidden from even close inspection, but, when he turned a small, secret crank, their port-holes dropped open, and they were ready!

Wentworth smiled thinly as he manipulated that crank. By this dim light, and in the fog, it would be impossible to shoot accurately—but when the dawn began to thrust out of the sea ahead, and before the light grew too brilliant for his weak eyes, he would strike. The Spider would strike!

Wentworth settled back to his operation of the plane. He could no longer see the ship below, but the heavy thunder of its engines hammered through his own muted exhaust plainly enough, as long as he kept close. His speed would permit that, and there was nothing to do save wait. His gas tanks were full. They would last out the dawn, though they would be empty soon afterward. He would be forced to land far at sea after he had made his kill, and his boat was frail. Once more, Wentworth's lips curved slightly. It did not matter....

TIME DRAGGED past without meaning. Wentworth flew with half an eye on the instruments, his ears attuned to the beat of motors ahead. It was minutes after he flashed out of the fog into the clear brilliance of the moonlight night that he realized the change. He thrust himself more erectly in his seat and realized that his hand was trembling on the stick, that weakness ran through all his body like heat. He remembered his wound. It was well enough to boast bitterly that Blancos did not bleed, but that bullet had clawed through his side. He felt it numbly with his fingers, and pain throbbed wildly through him.

God, was he going to faint, to crash into the sea and let the chief get away, after all? Wentworth leaned forward weakly and peered down at the sea below. Far off to the east, he saw the lights of an ocean liner and below, and a quarter mile ahead, was the skimming great white form of the stolen clipper ship.

Wentworth dragged the throttle of his ship wide, felt it leap ahead. He felt fumblingly for the trips of his machine guns and cleared them with a short burst of fire. The heavy hammer of the weapons seemed to build strength within him, but it was strength of the mind alone. His brain seemed very clear. Probably he was bleeding some inside; his blood was thinner. It had worked that way with Dr. Rand.

Once more, Wentworth smiled slightly as he jockeyed to a position directly behind the seaplane. It had been cruelty to revive the man to a brief realization that he was a Blanco, but, by so doing, he had guaranteed that the atrocities of the chief would never again afflict the world! It was just. He would dive with blazing guns on the seaplane. Probably his own strength would last just long enough for that. Afterward… Well, no man could blame him if his hand failed at the controls. Nita… But Nita was gone, too.

Wentworth shoved the stick sharply forward, his eye on the cross-sights of his guns. Now they were on the tail of the great ship, reaching forward along the fuselage. Now, they were on the pilot's compartment—lead it by, say two yards… Wentworth shoved his thumbs hard home on the gun-trips, eased the stick forward again. All along the hull of the great sea-plane, he could spot the course of his tracers.

It was not Wentworth's will which pulled back the stick and lifted his amphibian out of its dive. It was years of flying experience, reflexes which would not be denied. The plane straightened out and Wentworth peered over the rim of cockpit. The seaplane was yawing drunkenly. One wing tipped low, lower— was abruptly snapped back into line. The devil, had he only wounded the pilot? Wentworth swung his plane about, but not in the tight virage he had planned. It swept wide and slow coming back.

The seaplane had leveled off, but it was settling toward the surface of the ocean like a great, wounded bird. The rattle of the motors, hitting irregularly, came to his ears, and abruptly they were cut. Furiously, Wentworth put his ship into a dive, again punched the trips of his guns and swept that long hull with bullets. The ship received them, and nothing changed. The ship still settled, gracefully, toward the sea. It struck, bounced, settled back, and abruptly dragged to a slow, washing glide across the sluggishly heaving waves.

Once more, Wentworth swept the hull with bullets. There was a rage in him that would not down. They must be killed, those murderers below. It was that rage which presently guided Wentworth to set his amphibian to the waters near the seaplane and taxi toward its wing-tip. It was almost more than he could contrive to fumble out of his seat and walk the wing of his ship as it drifted, engine cut off, to a slow collision with that out-stretched wing.

The tip of the amphibian crumpled on contact and Wentworth almost pitched into the sea, found himself sprawled on his stomach across the wing of the PanAmerican craft. Within the brilliantly lighted cabin, nothing stirred. Wentworth stared at it drunkenly and a deep, vibrating siren sounded in his ears. He twisted his head weakly and saw that he was within a quarter mile of the ocean liner he had seen long ago. Well, they shouldn't save the chief!

WENTWORTH'S ANGER drove him to his feet. He staggered along the wing toward the cabin of the ship, gun in hand. He had to hit the window three times before the glass shattered and he could thrust himself through. Men were sprawled in bloody attitudes of death. Ceiling, seats, windows were punctured in a score of places by his bullets. He bent over the bodies, fumbling with them, staring down at the dead faces. His lips twisted, half in pain, from his position.

He groped in his vest pocket and slid out his cigarette lighter,

159

stood staring at it through long moments before he thumbed open the base. Then he stooped and ground its base against the forehead of a dead man. When he straightened, the seal of the Spider glowed there as if etched in blood. Wentworth laughed crazily, straightened.

He looked into the muzzle of a leveled machine gun. The man in the door of the pilot's compartment was on his knees. Blood smeared his temple and ran its crazy tracery across his cheek, but his face was in brilliant light and Wentworth's eyes ached with it. He could not see.

"Still alive, Wentworth the man jeered. "Well, you won't be for long!"

Wentworth stared at him and the heavy gun in his right hand twitched, but did not rise. He stood no chance to raise it into line with that sub-machine gun bearing on him. Even a Blanco couldn't do that. He had to be sure when he fired. He would just be able to manage one shot. Wentworth's lips twisted back from his teeth.

"Still alive," he said hoarsely, "and still able to finish you off!"

The man laughed and there was the old sneering note in his voice. It was the chief all right.

"Wrong again, Wentworth," he said. "I'll burn you down. I can't fly this boat, but I can taxi it over the water and there's a ship waiting for me not more than a couple hundred miles away. I can make it soon after dawn. Wrong, you're the only man who knows my identity… Come to think of it, even you probably don't. Blancos can't see in light as bright as this." There was cold mockery in his voice.

160

Wentworth said slowly, "No, I can't see, but I know who you are." He was trying desperately to think. Somehow, he must distract the chief's attention long enough to lift the automatic and fire. After that… "I know who you are," he repeated thickly. "Major Hascomb was away from duty in Hillville without notice, and Major Hascomb has spent a good deal of time on Eastern service. Enough to be able to recognize Punjabi when it was spoken, as the chief did in the chamber where I was injected with the Blanco stuff." He paused.

"Allow me to congratulate you on your training of the whipmen. The way they fought was a credit to your military training—and drilling of them. Now, that trick of teaching Blancos to shoot, knowing that they were capable of high accuracy. Only an army man who had been in touch with races, inferior mentally, would have understood that capability. None of it would convict you, Major Hascomb—but it was enough for me."

"A great brain you have, Wentworth, even though you're a Blanco!" The man's sneer was goading, as if he wanted Wentworth to make the desperate attempt, wanted him to have the knowledge of his failure.

Wentworth laughed. "Yes, a great brain! But then you'd expect that of the Spider, wouldn't you?"

"The Spider!" Major Hascomb cried.

"Quite," Wentworth said. "Maybe you remember this Punjab proverb." He raised his voice, calling clearly. "Ram Singh, shoot this man through the shoulder—the right shoulder!"

Hascomb cursed and, for a brief moment, his head jerked toward the wing of the plane where Wentworth's ship still drifted. Wentworth could just see that. It was enough. He dropped to his knees and began shooting, shooting… He was not even aware when the automatic in his hand clicked empty. He was crawling toward Major Hascomb on his knees and finally he was above the man. He seized him by the throat, stared, and began to laugh. The seven bullets from his automatic had all grouped neatly in Hascomb's heart. Even as a purblind Blanco, he retained his skill with an automatic.

Once more, he dragged out the cigarette lighter, imprinted his seal, then staggered back to the window by which he had entered. Wentworth had no plan in mind. He was weak, reeling from his wound. The fight was over, a Blanco had triumphed over his master… He fumbled his way out of the window, stood swaying on the wing. He blinked incredulously. A boat from the liner was within a hundred feet of where he stood! It seemed to him that the wing on which he stood was slanting at a sharp angle toward the water. He knew that he was suddenly unable to maintain his footing. He slipped and the cold water clapped together over his head….

WITHOUT REALIZING it, he struggled to the surface. His head was very clear—damnably clear. This was a good end. He knew it was time to go. His work was done, a last monument to the Spider's name—and no one need know that he had died a Blanco. He was sinking again when a voice throbbed in his ears—a voice he knew.

"Dick!" it cried. "Dick, hold on a minute longer!"

Nita? Nita on that liner? Incredible! He was imagining things.

"Dick!" she cried. "Dick, don't let go—I can cure you! Doctor Lieberling—"

Wentworth strained his eyes. There was no light on the boat and he could see quite clearly. No, he was not wrong. That was Nita, and she said—she said Lieberling… Wentworth began to laugh and the water got into his throat. He was still laughing when he was hauled into the boat, just in time as the giant seaplane lurched heavily and the water began to pour in through its windows. Wentworth saw it go and realized dimly that his bullets must have punched holes through the bottom, too. It was madness to have put that Spider seal on Hascomb. Why, he was going to live, *to live*….

He gripped Nita's arm, and his voice came out fiercely. "That wasn't trickery, dearest," he whispered. "You didn't do that to—to make me go on living. That would be cruel!"

Nita's eyes were swimming with tears. "No, dearest. I got Kirkpatrick on the wireless phone. His men have rounded up the Blancos with whips and lights, he says. Doctor Lieberling thinks he may be able to save them all. Doctor Rand told him how, just before he died… Transfusions, a long series of them, and certain gland treatments."

Wentworth sat down weakly on a seat of the boat. He felt Nita's arms about him, lifting his head until he was gazing into her eyes.

"Your poor eyes," she whispered. "They'll be strong again, too."

Wentworth laughed exultantly, as his arms closed about her. "Strong, dear?" he said. "That's not why there are tears in my eyes, darling. Believe it or not—" he was whispering now—"there are times when even the Spider can cry!"

And she understood.

POPULAR HERO PULPS AVAILABLE NOW:

THE SPIDER
- ❑ #1: The Spider Strikes — $13.95
- ❑ #2: The Wheel of Death — $13.95
- ❑ #3: Wings of the Black Death — $13.95
- ❑ #4: City of Flaming Shadows — $13.95
- ❑ #5: Empire of Doom! — $13.95
- ❑ #6: Citadel of Hell — $13.95
- ❑ #7: The Serpent of Destruction — $13.95
- ❑ #8: The Mad Horde — $13.95
- ❑ #9: Satan's Death Blast — $13.95
- ❑ #10: The Corpse Cargo — $13.95
- ❑ #11: Prince of the Red Looters — $13.95
- ❑ #12: Reign of the Silver Terror — $13.95
- ❑ #13: Builders of the Dark Empire — $13.95
- ❑ #14: Death's Crimson Juggernaut — $13.95
- ❑ #15: The Red Death Rain — $13.95
- ❑ #16: The City Destroyer — $13.95
- ❑ #17: The Pain Emperor — $13.95
- ❑ #18: The Flame Master — $13.95
- ❑ #19: Slaves of the Crime Master — $13.95
- ❑ #20: Reign of the Death Fiddler — $13.95
- ❑ #21: Hordes of the Red Butcher — $13.95
- ❑ #22: Dragon Lord of the Underworld — $13.95
- ❑ #23: Master of the Death-Madness — $13.95
- ❑ #24: King of the Red Killers — $13.95
- ❑ #25: Overlord of the Damned — $13.95
- ❑ #26: Death Reign of the Vampire King — $13.95
- ❑ #27: Emperor of the Yellow Death — $13.95
- ❑ #28: The Mayor of Hell — $13.95
- ❑ #29: Slaves of the Murder Syndicate — $13.95
- ❑ #30: Green Globes of Death — $13.95
- ❑ #31: The Cholera King — $13.95
- ❑ #32: Slaves of the Dragon — $13.95
- ❑ #33: Legions of Madness — $12.95
- ❑ #34: Laboratory of the Damned — $12.95
- ❑ #35: Satan's Sightless Legion — $12.95
- ❑ #36: The Coming of the Terror — $12.95
- ❑ #37: The Devil's Death-Dwarfs — $12.95
- ❑ #38: City of Dreadful Night — $12.95
- ❑ #39: Reign of the Snake Men — $12.95
- ❑ #40: Dictator of the Damned — $12.95
- ❑ #41: The Mill-Town Massacres — $12.95
- ❑ #42: Satan's Workshop — $12.95
- ❑ #43: Scourge of the Yellow Fangs — $12.95
- ❑ #44: The Devil's Pawnbroker — $12.95
- ❑ #45: Voyage of the Coffin Ship — $12.95
- ❑ #46: The Man Who Ruled in Hell — $13.95
- ❑ #47: Slaves of the Black Monarch — $13.95
- ❑ #48: Machineguns Over the White House — $13.95
- ❑ #49: The City That Dared Not Eat — $13.95
- ❑ #50: Master of the Flaming Horde — $13.95
- ❑ #51: Satan's Switchboard — $13.95
- ❑ #52: Legions of the Accursed Light — $13.95
- ❑ #53: The City of Lost Men — $13.95
- ❑ **NEW:** #54: The Grey Horde Creeps — $13.95

THE WESTERN RAIDER
- ❑ #1: Guns of the Damned — $13.95
- ❑ #2: The Hawk Rides Back from Death — $13.95
- ❑ #3: Gun-Call for the Lost Legion — $13.95
- ❑ #4: The Law of Silver Trent — $13.95
- ❑ #5: The Gun-Prayer of Silver Trent — $13.95
- ❑ #6: Silver Trent Rides Alone — $13.95

G-8 AND HIS BATTLE ACES
- ❑ #1: The Bat Staffel — $13.95

CAPTAIN SATAN
- ❑ #1: The Mask of the Damned — $13.95
- ❑ #2: Parole for the Dead — $13.95
- ❑ #3: The Dead Man Express — $13.95
- ❑ #4: A Ghost Rides the Dawn — $13.95
- ❑ #5: The Ambassador From Hell — $13.95

DR. YEN SIN
- ❑ #1: Mystery of the Dragon's Shadow — $12.95
- ❑ #2: Mystery of the Golden Skull — $12.95
- ❑ #3: Mystery of the Singing Mummies — $12.95

POPULAR HERO PULPS **AVAILABLE NOW:**

CAPTAIN COMBAT
- ❏ #1: The Sky Beast of Berlin — $13.95
- ❏ *NEW:* #2: Red Wings For the Blood Battalion — $13.95

CAPTAIN ZERO
- ❏ #1: City of Deadly Sleep — $13.95
- ❏ #2: The Mark of Zero! — $13.95
- ❏ #3: The Golden Murder Syndicate — $13.95

OPERATOR 5
- ❏ #1: The Masked Invasion — $13.95
- ❏ #2: The Invisible Empire — $13.95
- ❏ #3: The Yellow Scourge — $13.95
- ❏ #4: The Melting Death — $13.95
- ❏ #5: Cavern of the Damned — $13.95
- ❏ #6: Master of Broken Men — $13.95
- ❏ #7: Invasion of the Dark Legions — $13.95
- ❏ #8: The Green Death Mists — $13.95
- ❏ #9: Legions of Starvation — $13.95
- ❏ #10: The Red Invader — $13.95
- ❏ #11: The League of War-Monsters — $13.95
- ❏ #12: The Army of the Dead — $13.95
- ❏ #13: March of the Flame Marauders — $13.95
- ❏ #14: Blood Reign of the Dictator — $13.95
- ❏ #15: Invasion of the Yellow Warlords — $13.95
- ❏ #16: Legions of the Death Master — $13.95
- ❏ #17: Hosts of the Flaming Death — $13.95
- ❏ #18: Invasion of the Crimson Death Cult — $13.95
- ❏ #19: Attack of the Blizzard Men — $13.95
- ❏ #20: Scourge of the Invisible Death — $13.95
- ❏ #21: Raiders of the Red Death — $13.95
- ❏ #22: War-Dogs of the Green Destroyer — $13.95
- ❏ #23: Rockets From Hell — $13.95
- ❏ #24: War-Masters from the Orient — $13.95
- ❏ #25: Crime's Reign of Terror — $13.95
- ❏ #26: Death's Ragged Army — $13.95
- ❏ #27: Patriots' Death Battalion — $13.95
- ❏ #28: The Bloody Forty-five Days — $13.95
- ❏ #29: America's Plague Battalions — $13.95
- ❏ *NEW:* #30: Liberty's Suicide Legions — $13.95

DUSTY AYRES AND HIS BATTLE BIRDS
- ❏ #1: Black Lightning! — $13.95
- ❏ #2: Crimson Doom — $13.95
- ❏ #3: The Purple Tornado — $13.95
- ❏ #4: The Screaming Eye — $13.95
- ❏ #5: The Green Thunderbolt — $13.95
- ❏ #6: The Red Destroyer — $13.95
- ❏ #7: The White Death — $13.95
- ❏ #8: The Black Avenger — $13.95
- ❏ #9: The Silver Typhoon — $13.95
- ❏ #10: The Troposphere F-S — $13.95
- ❏ #11: The Blue Cyclone — $13.95
- ❏ #12: The Tesla Raiders — $13.95

MAVERICKS
- ❏ #1: Five Against the Law — $12.95
- ❏ #2: Mesquite Manhunters — $12.95
- ❏ #3: Bait for the Lobo Pack — $12.95
- ❏ #4: Doc Grimson's Outlaw Posse — $12.95
- ❏ #5: Charlie Parr's Gunsmoke Cure — $12.95

THE MYSTERIOUS WU FANG
- ❏ #1: The Case of the Six Coffins — $12.95
- ❏ #2: The Case of the Scarlet Feather — $12.95
- ❏ #3: The Case of the Yellow Mask — $12.95
- ❏ #4: The Case of the Suicide Tomb — $12.95
- ❏ #5: The Case of the Green Death — $12.95
- ❏ #6: The Case of the Black Lotus — $12.95
- ❏ #7: The Case of the Hidden Scourge — $12.95

THE SECRET 6
- ❏ #1: The Red Shadow — $13.95
- ❏ #2: House of Walking Corpses — $13.95
- ❏ #3: The Monster Murders — $13.95
- ❏ #4: The Golden Alligator — $13.95

www.ingramcontent.com/pod-product-compliance
Lightning Source LLC
Chambersburg PA
CBHW052134170626
46812CB00004B/1413